PASSING LINCOLN

*Small gifts
in the right Hands
go a long way.*

Michael S. Rogers

Published in Flora, Indiana, by A2G Media.

Scripture quotations are from the ESV® Bible (The Holy Bible, English Standard Version®). Copyright 2001 by Crossway, a publishing ministry of Good News Publishers. All Rights Reserved.

ISBN # 987-1-7327500-0-5

For Dan and Christina Sands,
Chris and Michelle Waggoner,
Nathan and Sarah Gilstrap,
Scott and Jessica Mattingly.

You believed when others did not.

ACKNOWLEDGMENTS

Writing a book can seem a lonely endeavor. In reality, the author is never alone even when running his fingers across the keyboard late at night. His family is giving him the space he needs — thank you, my beautiful wife Carrie and four amazing kids, Elijah, Anna, Caitlin, and Nathan. His extended family is waiting to get a copy to help with the editing — thank you, Tina Brison & Jeni Rogers (two of my genius sisters) and Chad Wilkinson (my writer brother-in-law).

His friends and fans come along after, helping him finalize the copy the publisher gets to see; reading it first, giving brutally honest feedback, reviewing and posting to spread the word. I'm deeply indebted to my Launch Team:

Amber Richardson, Krista Mayo, Heather Blanton, Julie Newlin, Dave Falkenberg, Tammy Scott, Sydney Wiles, Tina Miller, Robin Faith, Shelly Wiles, Jessica Burnett, Beth Glover, Chris Purvis, Sandi Baete, David Sekanic, K T Brison, Leslie Huckstep, Dean Eller, Emily Wagoner, and Karli Spesard.

I can't forget my final Launch Team member, Natalie Newlin, who also put together the cover design (she rocks at everything she does).

Last, but not least, the two guys named Andy at other publishing houses who helped me stick to my guns. Thank you all.

PROLOGUE: FATHER

He thinks no one understands, but I do.

Chet Spaulding was named after his great grandfather. He hates having an old person's name, but he once loved being called Little Chet. Already, he's planning on going by his middle name, Dylan, when he goes to college. For now, LC is his compromise with his parents.

Sitting in the back seat of his father's car, LC fumes about missing a party last night. His parents, Bobby and Sally, kept him home for the night so he wouldn't miss visiting Gran today. He doesn't know this saved him from tragedy. He only knows he missed out on a birthday party with his friends.

LC turned seventeen yesterday. His friends intended to line up shots for each year — the first sixteen tequila but the last, heroin. He doesn't know this because I prompted his parents to keep him home. He could have gone anyway, but he didn't. I love LC so much.

The car pulls in the driveway as Dolores Joyce stands at the window. She holds an envelope in shaky hands. Her grey curls are not as tight as they were earlier in the month. They would grow out more now that she chose to give her salon money to LC for his birthday. She thinks it's a small sacrifice, but I know it's greater than she can imagine. I love Dolores so much.

Sally gets out of the car, angry. She's asking LC to be excited about seeing his great grandmother. What she really wants is to be loved by her son, by her husband, by her grandmother-in-law. She just isn't sure why anyone would love her, so she tries too hard to make them. She turns and bends down to look at her son through the tinted window.

"Chester Dylan Spaulding, you get out of the car right now!"

Her heart is in the right place, but it is bruised. What she thinks is loving is not perceived as loving by LC (who turns away) or Bobby (who bristles) or Dolores (who wilts, thinking LC doesn't want to see her). Her intention doesn't change the hurt she has caused all three out of her insecurity. I love Sally so much.

Bobby says, "Sally!" with more edge than he intends and she backs down from his authority. He doesn't know he has wounded her again because he is blinded by frustration with the two people he loves most.

He turns to his son in the back seat, red from his neck across his face past the white wings at his temples and into the scalp beneath the gelled spikes of dark brown hair. He uses what he calls his father voice — which is less fatherly and more dictatorial — to tell his son he will get out of the car this instant or face consequences.

He is too hard on a teenager who is already vulnerable. I love Bobby so much.

Sighing, LC dons a mask of indifference. When he gets out of the car, Dolores sees the stone-cold expression through the blinds, confirming her fear. The envelope shakes more visibly. To give her hands work, she sets the envelope on the dining table next to the gel pen she used earlier to write on the card and the five-dollar bill. She goes to the refrigerator and pulls out sandwich meat and condiments.

LC leaves his car door open on purpose, hiding beneath blonde bangs as he passes his mother and goes to the front door. Sally glares at Bobby before closing her son's door and then her own. Sliding out from under the steering wheel, Bobby prays for a little help. He doesn't expect Me to listen, but I smile as they approach a turning point in their lives and their faith. I've already answered that prayer. I love them so much.

Sally and Chet wait for Bobby to approach and knock on the door. As soon as Dolores answers, Sally smothers her with love and affection. She's hoping the tension isn't noticeable. More importantly, she's hoping to atone for the harsh words Dolores heard earlier. Of course, My aging little saint has forgiven her already. I anticipate giving her a new body and seeing her dance again.

LC walks by with a courteous nod and plops down in the easy chair. Dolores worries about how small the apartment is, but she needn't. Her three guests are more focused on LC than on her living arrangements. Sally sits on the far end of the couch as Bobby swallows Gran with a hug.

"How's my girl feeling?"

"Like mashed potatoes right this minute," Gran says. The three of us chuckle at that. When Bobby pulls back, his brown eyes catch her emerald greens to let her know he knows. She pats his cheek and says, "Anyone hungry?"

LC feels bad that he didn't give Gran a hug. He knows she loves to share things with them, so he says, "Yes, please."

Sally misinterprets and is about to say something, but Bobby is walking toward them and cuts her off. He says, "It speaks!"

"You leave that young man alone," Gran says. "He said please, and that means he has better manners than you. Black forest ham or roast beef?"

"Ham, please," LC says, a hint of a smile at the corner of his mouth. It draws Dolores' attention to the lip ring and the bit of dark scruff on his chin, but she just smiles back.

Did I mention how much I love her?

She walks over to the pantry and pulls out some potato chips and bread. Setting them on the counter, she starts on the ham sandwich. LC says yes to cheese and mayo, and Bobby says he'll have the same. Sally tries to prepare the meal for Gran, then tries to say no to food to save Gran some money. Dolores will have none of either.

The three sit down at the dining table, Bobby with his back to the front window, Sally across from him. LC sits down with his back to the front door. The envelope holding his birthday card is on the table near the center.

The birthday boy wants to open it but he pretends he can't see it.

4

Gran puts plates down in front of everyone and pours lemonade into some plastic cups. They engage in small talk, but Dolores sees the envelope and can't hide her anxiety. She asks Me to help her say the right things when the time comes. I smile and remain silent.

The meal is almost over when Sally notices the envelope. "Oh, Gran, you shouldn't have."

"What a blessing, LC!" Bobby's recovery doesn't make up for Sally's mistake, but Dolores is such a forgiving woman. She knows instinctively that Sally desires to help, not to hurt. Besides, she is too nervous to think of more than what might happen when Little Chet opens his present.

Pulling it to him, LC runs a finger under the flap and releases the card from the envelope. Dark blue with a lighter "17" across the entire face, the card says *Happy birthday, grandson!* and shows the silhouette of a teenager in a ball cap jumping in celebration, arms raised. It's cheesy to him, but it makes him smile. To Gran, his smile looks like a smirk because she is so nervous.

He opens the card and two bills fall out—a twenty and a five. The twenty is on top, but the five slips out from under it, showing the face of Abraham Lincoln. LC knows a little about the cost of this gift for Gran, so he holds it up for his parents to see. When he does, the sunlight from the window shows through the bills and he notices some writing on the back of the five. I should admit, I made sure the clouds were not in the way at this moment.

Turning the bill over, he sees the Lincoln Memorial. At the top in all caps is THE UNITED STATES OF AMERICA. Under it are the words IN GOD WE TRUST. Gran has underlined my name with the gel pen and drawn a line to her message.

You can too, LC.

Such a simple effort. I am pleased by this effort, but LC is confused. He can trust God, too? For what? Why does she care what he believes? He thinks for a moment of his childhood and how he was raised on stories of Me and My Son, but they feel far away. His parents have tried for years to bring him back to faith, but he doesn't know what to think.

LC realizes all eyes are on him. He looks up at his great grandmother, careful not to reveal what he is thinking. Gran's lips press thin. Dad arches an eyebrow and Mom wrings her hands.

"Gran," he finally says, "if there is a God, He can use this five-dollar bill to reach me. Right?"

"Yes."

Reaching for the gel pen, LC grips it and writes on the back under Gran's message. He stands up, grabbing the twenty and leaving the card, the envelope, and the five on the table. Without looking back, he opens the front door and says, "I'll be in the car."

Sally gushes with apologies. Bobby thanks Gran for the gift. Dolores retrieves the five and reads what LC wrote. Her heart wilts and she asks Me to bless her great grandson. LC opens the car door and slips in the backseat, mad at himself, at Gran, and his parents. All of them believe this is a catastrophic moment.

I know better. Because of the gift, I get to change their lives. I love them, but I also love Lianne and Jack and Matthew and Chris and all the rest.

Now, to show them how much.

DOLORES

The melody washed over her, whispering truth as the people stood all around her and sang. Dolores Joyce was satisfied to remain in her seat and let her soul do the rising. Her legs were not as steady as they used to be.

Funny, how important it once was to lift her voice. Lost somewhere between alto and soprano, her lack of talent and training did nothing to deter the gusto with which she sang the hymns. *The Old Rugged Cross. All to Jesus. Lead Me to Calvary. Amazing Grace.* At one time, worship meant singing loudly to prove to others the strength of her conviction.

She had learned better. Too many people spent much of their worship on singing and little of it on life. Wisdom, hope, grace, truth; often, these beautiful gifts of God came in the spaces between. Perhaps she was mellowing with age — she turned eighty last year — but lately, her adoration was best served by silence. Dolores smiled as the young man on the stage caressed six strings devoted to his Lord, sharing this moment of worship as intimately as she once shared with her husband.

Force of habit made her pat the pew beside her where Chet's feathery hand should lay. He always sat on her right near the end because he never knew when his restless legs would act up. He was a thoughtful man. Chet had gone to Glory seventeen years ago. Pity, she thought to herself. He would have loved Jason's way with a guitar.

Closing emerald eyes to focus on the song, she imagined her great grandson was the young man up there singing a baritone version of *Because He Lives*. Little Chet, her husband's namesake, turned seventeen on Friday. He had inherited her devilish grin and Old Chet's stubbornness. Dolores shook her grey head a little as if to rattle the thought around so it fell from one of her failing ears.

Her hand missed Old Chet's. The serenity of the moment evaporated. LC took after his great grandfather in many ways, but the one glaring difference meant everything to Dolores. Chester Joyce was spending eternity with Jesus. If his namesake knew how much it would weigh on Old Chet's mind, would Little Chet listen to him?

Probably not. Sherrilynn had been their most wayward child, and Bobby had been hers. The poor boy came from a long line of *I don't want to*. Were Chet alive, LC would have run from Jesus just to get under his great grandfather's skin.

If Chet were alive, though, Little Chet would have been Dylan Spaulding. Bobby and Sally had honored Dolores by naming LC after her husband when he died of a heart attack a week before their son was born. She chuckled. LC was probably mad at her because he had to grow up with an old person's name. Dylan would have been way cooler, as the kids would say. Did they say that anymore?

Well, he might be mad at her for more than that. Her left hand opened, finally releasing what she had been clutching since the night before. Bobby and Sally had brought LC over to her home so she could give him a present for his birthday. With access to all the amazing technology of the day, Dolores had no idea what passed as a good gift for a teenager. Years before, she gave up guessing and started stuffing cards with the only thing that never lost value to a young person: cash.

LC was seventeen — had Chet been gone that long? — so she put twenty-five dollars in the card. She couldn't afford more. Her monthly check allowed her to give God His and pay her bills and not much else. Dolores was not a woman for vices. She didn't smoke or drink or play bingo at the Knights of Columbus. Her only guilty pleasure was a monthly trip to the beauty salon. For LC, she could wait to get her hair done. What a silly, small sacrifice it seemed if she found a way to talk to her great-grandson about God.

Pulling each end until the bill was tight, she looked down at the distinguished Abraham Lincoln gracing the front. How hard it once was to earn this much money. Now, she was giving it away for birthdays and adding a twenty to boot.

Only, her gift had not been as arbitrary as that. The impression of the writing on the other side of the bill created the illusion of extra wrinkles just above Lincoln's eyebrow. She wished now she hadn't used one of those gel pens. They showed through so easily, and hadn't she felt guilty enough breaking the law by defacing it in the first place?

The song had changed without her notice. Standing beside her, sweet young Mary Parkinson looked down to see why she wasn't singing. Returning to the moment, Dolores recognized *When I Survey the Wondrous Cross*, Chet's absolute favorite. Of all the songs to choose today, when she was so distracted.

With difficulty, Dolores met Mary's cow-brown eyes and blinked back a swell of emotion. Thinking she understood, Mary cupped both hands under her blue dress to smooth the white polka dots out of her way before she sat down.

"You still miss him, don't you?"

Well, what could she say to that? "Yes."

"I love you, Mrs. Joyce."

Dolores took a hand away from Mister Lincoln and patted Mary's. She couldn't say anything. Grabbing the girl's wrist, she pulled up on it until Mary stood again with the rest of them. Mary trapped a wisp of red hair behind her ear and gave Dolores a wink before rejoining the congregation.

Looking back down, Dolores stared at the Great Man who graced the front of the bill. The harsh lines on his face were too like Chet's, so she turned him face down. He retreated to an impression of himself sitting amid his own memorial. Over the building along the top of the note, "THE UNITED STATES OF AMERICA," and under it, "IN GOD WE TRUST." A dash pointed to her own looping penmanship and what she had put on there for LC to read after he walked out of the house. Only, he had seen it too soon.

Chet would have been disappointed if she hadn't tried. Jesus, too, she supposed. She invoked the words beneath the music and the singing of her church family. *You can, too, LC.* Not much of a Gospel message. How else could she get a word into the mind of her great grandson? Every edge and angle in his boyish face screamed, "Don't touch me!" She couldn't just tell him Jesus loves him. Bobby and Sally had said that for years and he never listened to them. Maybe, she thought, he could entertain the notion that there is a God and He can be trusted.

Perhaps the gel pen gave her away. He opened the card, held up the two bills for his parents to see, and paused to inspect them. Her heart stopped as he turned Mister Lincoln face down and read what she had written there. What had she feared so much? That he would be angry? Would he storm out of the house and never return?

LC's mop of wavy blonde hair swung around in front of bright blue eyes, the bangs stark contrast to the dark scruff on his chin. His teeth were already starting to yellow (from cigarettes?). His hands were soft (weak, Chet would have said) but his heart was fiercely uncompromising. Dolores held her breath as he separated the five from the twenty and stared at her inscription. When he looked up, she couldn't read his eyes.

"Gran," he finally said, "if there is a God, He can use this five-dollar bill to reach me. Right?"

Well, what could she say to that? "Yes."

How long had it been since her heart hammered in her breast just so? Even Bobby held his breath as he looked at his son. LC turned Mister Lincoln up so he could see the room again, then met his gaze unflinchingly. The world stopped spinning, like when Joshua needed more time to defeat the five kings of the Amorites.

Looking over, LC saw the gel pen on the table in front of him. He picked it up and laid the note down. After thinking for a moment, he bent and scribbled something on it.

"I'll be in the car," he said to the front door.

An unflattering thought entered Dolores' mind as the screen door rattled the jamb. Would he have left it like that if she had written on the twenty? Sally retrieved the money for her, apologizing, saying she knew how hard it was to give this money, what with her situation and all. Dolores wasn't listening. She was waiting to find out what LC had written.

"Some glad morning, when this life is o'er, I'll fly away!"

The sudden increase in tempo jarred her back to the present. Pastor Preston loved to have exciting music right before they took up the offering. He was a young preacher, new to the ministry. In a few years, he would learn it didn't matter what song played when the church asked for more money. People gave what they gave.

Dolores pulled the folded check out of the pocket of her flower print dress with her left hand and clutched the five with her right. Mister Lincoln was face down in the peonies on her knee, which allowed LC's jagged response to stare up at her. She closed her eyes against it.

"Let's celebrate God now with our giving," Jason said. "Will the ushers please pass the plate as we sing this song? It's a little newer than the ones we usually sing, but I think you'll like it. It's called . . ."

The melody was provocative, sweet and yet strong enough to get Dolores Joyce's attention. She would learn to love it later, but for the moment all she could hear was LC's hopeless tone. He wasn't angry or bitter or unforgiving. No, what he was feeling was much worse: indifference. She asked God what she could do. An old woman, unable to find the right words, unable to speak them if she did. Had she thought those few words on the back of some money could matter? Was she past the age where God could use her to reach anyone?

The two young men passing the plate stood on either end of the row in front of hers. Looking down, she turned Mister Lincoln over so he could see her again. She wondered if she could still get her hair done if she kept him.

Glaring at the picture, she saw again the shadows on his brow caused by the gel pen. They made him look stern. They weren't wrinkles, they were creases caused by a determination that carried him through the worst years of American history.

What had sustained him? His faith that God alone knew what was best. How fitting, that right behind his head on every note was the phrase, "In God we trust." *Do they, anymore? Do you, Dolores?*

Of course, Mister Lincoln hadn't spoken to her; but he stared back, daring her to prove her faith. A bark of laughter escaped her, very unladylike.

Sitting beside her, Mary glanced with concern. Dolores raised her hand and shook her head to let Mary know she didn't need assistance. Not crazy, sweet young Mary, just having an imaginary faith face-off with a dead president.

The usher was about to receive the plate and she would soon be giving her tithe to God. Was that enough? Just give Him more resources and hope someone eventually reached these young kids? Not many came to their church. Dolores didn't have to look around to know that Mary was the youngest person other than the Dawson twins. When Blaise Dawson had her little one — out of wedlock, but that wasn't uncommon nowadays — the baby would be the first addition to the flock since Eunice died and Jason replaced her organ with his guitar last February.

The plate was in the usher's hand and he was turning to give it to her. What was it LC had asked her? If she believed a five-dollar bill could save him? Before she could reconsider, Dolores took the plate and tossed the check and Mister Lincoln into it.

No going back now. Who puts money in the church offering and then asks for it back later? The chance for a hair appointment was gone. The chance to keep the five in hopes of further conversation with LC was gone. Whatever happened to it now, only God knew.

The urge to pray came over her so strongly that tears leaked from her eyes.

"Oh, God," she whispered. "If you're there, if you're really there, you can use my money to save one of those kids. I don't want to be selfish. It doesn't have to be my Little Chet. Whoever it is, God, I pray you use my gift to help them see Jesus."

Dolores put her face in her hands. She didn't know she was crying out loud until Mary Parkinson was holding her shaking shoulders.

Mister Lincoln's companions were scant as the usher received the plate from the last person. James Randolph was a deacon at the church and had been collecting the offering for over twenty years. As he walked to the back of the sanctuary to meet his other ushers, he straightened his collar and freed his tie. Had he ever seen a smaller amount of money on Sunday morning? His plate easily received the pittance from the other three trays. None of the ushers made eye contact with him.

Will joined him as they took the funds out the double doors from the sanctuary that led to the fellowship room. Turning right, they walked down the short hall and entered the church office on their left. Pastor Preston would begin his sermon shortly, but it wasn't like they never heard a sermon on the first chapter of Ephesians before. Besides, the counting wouldn't take long.

James emptied the plate onto the desk. After separating them from the cash, his partner recorded each check for the giving statements at the end of the year. He noticed with satisfaction that Dolores Joyce was still tithing despite her perilous financial situation. Some of the other elderly people were not so faithful.

In the middle of counting, James noticed one of the five-dollar bills had scribbling on it. He couldn't read the scrawl very well, but the script on the side was certainly Dolores' hand. *You can too, LC.* Bless that girl's heart. Must be Little Chet who wrote the note under IN GOD WE TRUST. What did it say? You can . . . if? . . . You can if you want to.

"Whatcha got there, Jim?"

"Will, how long you known me?"

Will smiled. "Sorry. What's that in your hand, James?"

"I think it's a Dear John letter to God."

"A what?"

James reached into his suit pants and pulled out his wallet. "Watch me do this, will you?"

As Will looked on, James exchanged a ten for the five. He put Mister Lincoln in his front pocket and patted him down. His partner deacon looked at him like he was crazy, and maybe he was. He had no idea what he planned to do with it. James Randolph just knew he couldn't let it go to the bank and disappear there.

After church, James took his family out to eat and invited Dolores Joyce to join them. He meant to give her back the five but forgot and tipped the waitress with it instead. She was such a sweet girl. He'd never given any of the serving staff that much before, but she deserved it. Not because she was a good waitress — he reminded her twice to bring him the free coffee he always demanded after the meal — but because he knew her, knew she had a baby at home who would never know his daddy.

Who knows? Maybe five dollars was enough to bless someone after all.

LIANNE

Not until she closed the car door did she realize how much she smelled like day-old Mexican food. For once, she didn't mind. Normally, Sunday afternoon shift was penance for doing something the management didn't like. Lianne Wallace had been a server for five years and knew better than anyone why they called Sunday lunch the *Church Lurch*: demanding people who left tracts about Jesus and a fifty-cent tip for a thirty-dollar ticket. "Gold and silver I do not have . . ." one of them had written on a napkin once after feeding his family of seven at ten dollars a plate.

Li always picked up the shift from other servers she knew needed more money. She was a Christian herself and believed God would take care of her despite giving up a good shift once or twice a month. Besides, she didn't have any other way to give money to people who needed it. Her baby girl depended on her and money was always tight. Taking a bad shift was her offering when she couldn't afford to give.

21

Li pumped the gas pedal twice, stroked the dashboard, and turned the key. The old Ford Taurus whined and spit at her, then rumbled to life. She waited for the puff of exhaust to clear before checking her rearview mirror. All clear. Carefully feathering the gas and brake to keep the engine running without crashing into anything, Li backed out of her parking space and steered toward Wal-Mart. She was smiling because today, for some reason, the tips were excellent. She had budgeted to make thirty but for some reason was bringing home about ninety dollars. No, not for some reason — Her God had supplied her needs.

The light was green when she made it to the intersection and under her breath, she whispered, "Praise Jesus." She turned left into the bright summer sun still hovering well above the horizon. Less chance of the Old Green Monster dying than if in winter, but she got caught in the middle of a turn in an intersection without power steering before. Highway 58 was the main commercial strip in Beulah, Indiana. Wal-Mart was stationed on the north side between its favorite allies — McDonald's, Sam's Club, Lowe's, and myriad car dealerships and auto shops. Across the highway was the entrenched competition — Home Depot, Office Depot, Kmart, Burger King, and myriad hobby shops from gardening to comic books.

The two armies faced off, cars like precious cattle lining the parking lots that separated them. A steady stream of traffic made a watery barrier that kept either side from crossing over except to send occasional spies for groceries or copy paper, the convenience of price or layaway. Li chose sides, opting for groceries and price as she turned north.

The radio no longer worked in the old boat, so she hummed a Chris Tomlin tune about how awesome God is. Checking her cell phone for the time, she rolled to a stop to let another car in front of her. The engine died. She pulled a strand of brunette hair back behind her ear. No need to pump the pedal again, so she shifted to neutral, stroked the dash, turned the key, and continued on. Caitie Beth needed to be picked up in an hour. She had plenty of time to get food.

Navigating all the little islands in the parking lot, Li grinned. Almost two, Caitie was just forming coherent sentences. Oh, she had been "talking" for a while; jabbering on and gesturing like her mommy, expecting everyone to know what she was saying. Rita was concerned that she wasn't talking better yet, but Li wasn't worried. Caitie Beth had a mind of her own, even at two—especially at two—and she would talk when she was ready. Rita was a good friend, though, to care so much.

Wal-Mart was especially busy. Li turned to cross in front of the store, looking for empty parking spaces down the next row as she did. A Hyundai SUV jumped out in front of her and she had to hit the brakes hard to avoid it. The Taurus sputtered and died again. Looking at the bumper of the offending vehicle to avoid glaring at the driver, Li saw a sticker there that read, "Practice random acts of kindness and senseless acts of beauty."

She snorted as she put the car in neutral again, stroked the dash, turned the key. It whined a little, but the sound was thick and slow. Coasting, she took a deep breath, stroked the dash twice, and turned the key again. Nothing. The Ford crawled in front of the Wal-Mart exit.

An older lady with a full basket smiled and mouthed *thank you* as she pushed her cart in front of Li's car. She had no choice but to stop the car completely.

"Please God please God please," Li whispered as she straightened her ponytail. The weathered dash stroked, Li added a tug on the cross necklace hanging from the rearview mirror. Turned the key. Nothing. A car horn caused her to look past the necklace and into the mirror. A big pickup truck filled it, a heavy redheaded guy with grey in his red beard said, "Come on!" as he slammed the steering wheel with his fist.

Li put her face in her hands and bit her lip to force back tears. Taking a deep breath, she tried the key again. Nothing.

"This can't be happening," she prayed. "Not right in front of Wally World."

What now? The guy behind her honked his horn again, but she didn't look up. Not only was she blocking him, she also blocked the incoming lane. The Taurus was too big for her to push by herself and one more try with the key told her it was never going to start again. How would she pick up her daughter? If she was late again, she would probably lose her babysitter. The guy honked, longer this time, as if that would get her car started. Li pulled the scrunchie out of her chestnut hair and let it fall around her shoulders.

"You okay?"

She jumped and put her hands up defensively. Li had forgotten her window was down, so no glass separated her from the scruffy chin and doe brown eyes of the man standing there. He was a little older than her, but not by much, muscular shoulders escaping the sleeves of his tank top.

He had soft features, dark brown hair, and freckles on his nose. She recognized the driver who should be threatening to T-bone her from the parking lane perpendicular to her very dead car. Great.

"Sorry," he said, smiling. "I thought you saw me coming."

"I didn't." Stupid thing to say.

"I got a couple of buddies in the car. You need a push?"

"Oh, thank you."

The stranger turned and waved his buddies out of the sedan, two teenagers with hair in their eyes and arms too long for their torsos. A third teenager got in the driver's seat, ready to follow. When the boys got behind the car, the young man turned back to the window and smiled again.

"All right, we're gonna go straight until we get to the last row, and then put you in a spot. We can check out the car after we free up the traffic flow. You stay put and steer, okay?"

Li nodded and thanked God for sending someone who did more than random acts of kindness. The two boys didn't look very strong, but she could tell by how soon and how quickly the car rolled that they were. Thirty seconds of panic turned into thirty seconds of relief, ending in a spot on a flat space in the parking lot. When she put the Ford in park, she sighed. At least she was out of the way.

"I'm Jason," the young man said, extending a hand.

"Lianne," she replied, tentatively accepting the handshake.

"What happened back there?"

"I don't know," she said. "It's been running rough for a while, but it stalled and then I couldn't get it started again."

25

One of the teenagers came up to the window. "Didn't sound like it was trying to start."

"Yeah, right. I was turning the key, but nothing was happening."

"That's her battery."

Jason nodded, then turned to her. "I know we just met, but do you trust me enough to run your battery over there?" Lianne looked to where he pointed and saw an auto parts place. "They'll check the battery for free."

"Why don't I go with you?"

"Great idea," he said. He opened the car door for her as if they had arrived at a restaurant to share dinner. Ludicrous thought. She got out and stepped back so he could reach in and release the hood. The third teen had freed a toolbox out of the trunk of Jason's car and brought it over.

"We're gonna miss the start of the game," one of the boys whined, looking at his cell.

Jason looked around the hood as he loosened one of the cables. "Come on, Seth. People are more important than baseball, right?"

Seth didn't look convinced, but he nodded.

Using a dirty towel that also came from his trunk, Jason wrapped the battery and then put it on a broad shoulder. "You ready?"

Li didn't look convinced, either; but she nodded, too. They walked over to the parts store in silence. Inside, she was a bit startled by the condition of the store. Used to the cleaner chain dealers, Lianne wondered if the place had ever been deep-cleaned. Not that it was grimy or dirty, just vaguely resembling the inside of a car engine.

Jason was unfazed by the environment. He marched to the counter and talked to the guy standing there. The man's name was Dave. He had jet black hair, creamy brown skin and the brightest smile she had ever seen. Jason got him to check the battery, then asked questions about the business. Dave the Auto Parts Guy was glad to talk about how insanely busy they had been since church let out.

"You go to church somewhere?"

Li glanced up, but Jason was talking to Dave, who said, "I'm usually here on Sundays."

"Would you go if church was Saturday night?"

"I heard about churches that do that. We have one here in town?"

"Not yet."

Dave laughed and Jason smiled. Dave squinted warily and said, "You the new pastor over at Beulah Community?"

"No, sir. But I just started leading worship there a couple months back."

Dave came out from behind the counter and they talked a while longer, but Li didn't hear much. She was too busy thanking Jesus for sending her someone she could trust. The bunched muscles in her shoulders relaxed a little. They resumed their tension when Dave turned to her and told her the battery was shot.

"How much is a new one?"

Dave said, "Well, you want to get one that you can rely on in winter." His face fell with hers, but then he brightened. "Don't worry, the cheapest one is on sale."

"How much?"

"$59.99, ma'am."

"What's wrong, Lianne?" Jason put his warm hand on her shoulder to turn her to him a little. His quizzical smile made her laugh out loud. "What's the matter?"

Lianne couldn't help herself. She hugged Dave and dug into her pocket. "God gave me sixty dollars today because He knew I'd need this battery!"

When she pulled out a wad of bills and placed them on the counter, the five on the top was turned face down and had writing on the back. Right next to where "IN GOD WE TRUST" was printed, someone had written, "You can, too, LC." Under that, in a younger scrawl, "You can if you want to."

Yes, she prayed silently. Yes, she could. Looking up at the man's name tag, she said, "Dave, do you have a pen I can borrow?"

With the borrowed pen, she underlined God and wrote under the scribble, "I do!"

Jason walked her back to her car and got the Taurus started again. He told her he thought he knew why it was dying and asked if he and his friends could help fix it. Before they parted company, he asked her to come to church. She decided that next week she would.

No time left for groceries, Lianne drove across town to pick up her daughter. She wasn't just humming a tune about her awesome God. She was singing with gusto.

DAVE

Subject: Need my Mama's ear for a minute
From: Dave Graybill
Date: 08/24/15 1:18 AM
To: Mom

Weird thing happened to me today, Mama. I can't talk to
Wendy about it yet, but I feel like I should talk to someone.
Talk. Well, I guess this email is talking. Don't feel like you
gotta reply, either. I'm just getting these thoughts out of my
head ☺

This young girl came into the store today with a young man.
His name is Jason, and he seems like a nice guy. He was
helping her fix her car and I sold them a cheap battery. Gave
them my discount, but don't tell the owner. He's not real keen
on charity!

I rang up the sale and started distributing the bills in their
proper slots in the cash register. Mostly ones, which is good.

Twenty years in retail has taught me to appreciate waitresses. Some young guys complain when they pay in ones, but they don't have to run to the bank to get change in the middle of a busy shift. Of course, if everybody paid in ones, we'd have to reconfigure the cash register.

Anyway, Jason is one of the music guys over at Beulah Community Church. He might have been trying to impress the waitress because I've seen her over at *Delicioso* a couple of times. Pretty, but you could tell life hadn't been simple for her. She wears a big cross necklace, but what does that mean today? Anyway, he might have been showing his "God side" to her, but he seemed sincere. Maybe an outgoing almost-preacher would be good for her.

Wow. Why is this so hard to get to? I promise I didn't write this email to discuss the glory of the dating scene in Beulah, Indiana.

This Jason guy asked me if I went to church anywhere. Well, you know how I feel about that. I've always kind of believed in God, and I think Jesus probably really lived and taught great things.

My idea of church, though, is getting out in the woods before dawn to wait on deer. It's so quiet and peaceful, I just can't imagine what God was thinking when he created humans. We screw everything up! When the sun breaks over the horizon, it's like the world is starting new again.

Don't tell Wendy, but I've had a couple of times when I've seen deer and couldn't shoot. I know we could use the meat, but they were more a part of the woods than me.

Anyway, Jason asked me if I go to church and I gave my "church is nature for me" speech. He listened to me, smiling the whole time, then asked me, "What is church, anyway?"

What kind of question is that? Don't he know? After all, he shows up at one every week evidently. That's why I think he was trying to impress the girl. He probably does play guitar at a church, but lead worship? Shouldn't he know what a church is to do that?

Except, his question has been bugging me ever since. What is church? You remember when Pop got religion for six months after he read that series of apocalypse books? He was scared to death and we all had to go to church every week until he was back to his old self. I guess I never understood why they looked so different and felt so much the same. What did we try, five or six? But one of them stands out. I bet you know which one I'm talking about.

No, not the one where the people eyed us like we were child molesters. Not the one where they ignored us, either. I'm talking about the one with the old, old preacher. What was his name? Brother Charles? They didn't have anything for the kids, so I had to sit in the sanctuary with you guys when he preached.

The people were kind enough. They didn't want us to leave and they didn't act like we weren't there. But I've met people as kind as them in bars and in the gym. What I remember most is that Brother Charles believed what he was saying. He didn't rail at us. He just talked to us about God. One of the things he told us was that he trusted God and that we could, too.

Well, that's why I'm writing you this email. I was putting away the money from that battery sale I mentioned. Jack was on break and no other customers were in the store. I counted the money again to be sure it was right. Thirty ones, two tens, two fives, and the rest in change made $64.19. As I put the last five in, I remembered the girl had written something on it.

Why do people do that to money? I remember one time hearing that every paper bill in American currency had a trace of drugs on it from being handled by junkies and dealers. That makes sense. But writing on a five-dollar bill? No sense at all. I flattened it out on the counter and leaned back a bit until it came into focus. Yeah, yeah, I know. I should be wearing glasses. Mrs. Graybill does enough nagging, and we've been married long enough for me to forgive her for it. You don't need to help her!

Anyway, I got myself positioned so I could read what it said. Someone had put a dash beside *In God we trust* and then wrote, "You can too, LC." Another person's handwriting was beneath that. "You can if you want to."

Maybe LC was responding, whoever he was, or maybe some random person had written it there in response. I chuckled. Serves the person right for trying to use money to talk about God. Doesn't it say something in the Bible about money being the root of all evil? Or maybe that was Pink Floyd…

Wait. You know who Pink Floyd is, right? ;-)

But then that girl had written "I do!" right underneath them. I suddenly had a flash back to Brother Charles. Didn't he always call the congregation, "Little Children"?! LC, you see? Okay, I just made myself "lol". So when I read the back of that five dollar bill, what I saw was:

In God we trust. You can too, Little Child. You can if you want to. I do!

Now, here's the weird part. I started thinking about Jason's question. What is church, anyway?

Maybe it's not what I thought it was. Maybe Brother Charles and Jason know something I don't. What if it has nothing to do with a weekly service, or a preacher and a collection plate, or Baptist or Methodist or Independent or Community or African Methodist Episcopal? What if it's all about people who trust God? Because if that's the case, why do they have to get together on Sunday morning, sing some old songs, and take donations? Didn't some of those churches eat a little cracker and drink a thimbleful of grape juice, too? Why do they do all that if the point is to trust God?

I'm spitballing now because I don't know much about church or God or anything. What if the reason they get together each week is actually supposed to be about learning to trust God? Was I too young to get that when I was a kid? Did you get that? I don't remember us ever stepping foot in a church again. I work on Sundays now, so don't think I'm suddenly going to get weird or religious (am I being redundant? ☺). I'm just wondering what you think about that.

Love you, Davey.

Subject: RE: Need my Mama's ear for a minute
From: Mamaw Graybill
Date: 08/24/15 8:41 AM
To: Davey

Funny that you sent that email last nite. Jeff and I started going to that old church last month. Brother Charles is dead, God rest his soul, but the preacher they have there now is as good. We met him at the Strawberry Festival about a year ago. Seemed like a nice young man. You knew Jeff was a Christian, right? Well, he said something about how if we ever got married it would be the next time he set foot in a church and most likely the last time.

You know I ain't going to marry him, right? I still feel your father with me. I can't believe he's gone. Anyway, Jeff is a nice man and he spoils me. I hope that don't make you uncomfortable. Silly, right? Worrying about trying to replace your boy's father when your boy is in his forties?

Anyway, the preacher smiled and asked *the exact same question your Jason kid did!* Can't be coincidence, can it? Well, quick as a whip, Jeff answered, "Church is the place where no one is welcome unless they've been there for years."

I slapped his shoulder and he turned and smiled like it was a joke. Ezra—he's the preacher—laughed. Laughed! Like Jeff hadn't insulted his whole reason for living.
So I said, "I'm sorry, Ezra. We just think the church is full of hypocrites." Know what he said? "Oh no, Ms. Graybill. There's room for two more."

I didn't know if I should be insulted, but I wasn't. He started talking about how church was people, real people, people who struggle the same way people do in (really, he even used the same two places you mentioned) in bars and gyms. He said people are people wherever you go, so if you go to a church you should expect people to be people. The difference in a church is that the people there are meeting on purpose to be with each other and with God.

I asked if people could do that without church, and he said, "Wherever people meet on purpose to be with each other and with God IS CHURCH." He said it's not the place or the events that make it church, but the purpose.

Well, that got us thinking. Maybe when your dad let those books talk him into taking us to church, we were so focused on the place and the events that we missed the purpose!

Hope that helps you understand better. We been kind of trying out praying, and one of the things we prayed recently is that our family would learn what we've learned about church. Maybe that makes this an answer to that prayer? I'm still new to this, but seems like it.

Love you, Mama. (P. S. I *introduced* you to Pink Floyd! ☺)

Subject: RE: Re: Need my Mama's ear for a minute
From: Dave Graybill
Date: 08/24/15 5:31 PM
To: Mom

Are you kidding me about Jeff? I told you last year you should marry the guy. Sounds like he's setting you on a good path, too. You're going to church now? Why didn't you tell me?

Jeff must have had a bad experience with church. I know a lot of people who have. After reading your email, I've been wondering if maybe the whole "bad church experience" is just an excuse to allow us not to go.

You know? Like, Jack gets on my nerves every other day, and I think he's stolen a few parts. But I put up with him. There are a couple guys at the gym I try to avoid, but I haven't stopped going just because I don't like them. And what would a good sports bar be without those belligerent fans who drink too much and yell too loudly at the game?

What your preacher friend said makes some sense.

What's worse, Wendy read your email over my shoulder so we had to talk about it. She thinks we should try Jason's church. We looked it up online and the service starts at 10. Even if they get crazy and go longer than I expect, I can get out of there and to the store in time to open at noon. It'll be just like when we went—nothing for my teenagers to do but sit with us. I hope it's entertaining.

Subject: Yay!
From: Mamaw Graybill
Date: 08/24/15 9:18 PM
To: Davey

Jeff and I are SOOO excited! Turns out Ezra knows that preacher there in Beulah Community. His name is Preston and he does a good job reaching young people. Tess and Alex will LOVE him. Tell them Mamaw says hello and I can't wait to see them for Thanksgiving!

Ain't it amazing what a five dollar bill can do?

Love, Mama.

JACK

What was up with Lance last night?

Pulling the cooler out of the passenger seat, Jack Ilsey opened the door of his new Mustang and unfolded his tall, gaunt frame into the warm sunshine. He pulled his cap off the short blond hair on his head and scratched at his scalp. Why had Lance been so weird? Jack did side jobs fixing cars — especially for friends — and they talked about replacing Lance's headlights because they were all fogged up. Lance kept calling them headlamps, but that wasn't what bugged Jack today.

What got under his skin was the God stuff. A new preacher started at Beulah Community and Lance was all excited about him. Even said his daughter Blaise was attending. Jack shook his head as he reached back into the car to disconnect his cell phone from the charger. Blaise was six months pregnant with her ex-boyfriend's child, and he heard the ex was a drug dealer. In Beulah, that was about as much scandal as one teenage girl could find.

After the fifth invitation, Jack smiled and said, "Lance, if God wanted me to be in church, He would give me some kind of sign."

"Isn't my asking a sign?"

"A different kind of sign."

"What kind?"

Snorting in frustration, Jack sized up his friend and said, "The kind where I'm absolutely certain He exists."

He couldn't get out of there fast enough after that, but he told Lance he'd get the "headlamps" and do the job that weekend. That's when Lance invited him for the sixth time. Some guys don't know when to give up.

Shrugging off the conversation, Jack closed the car door and did the three pats: phone, keys, wallet. Satisfied he had everything, he looked up at the front of the auto parts store where he worked. Tuesday mornings were Jack's favorite. He opened by himself, which made his other "side jobs" easier to manage. Too easy. If he did it every Tuesday morning, that tightwad Dave would start figuring him out. Jack picked a different Tuesday every month for his three favorite pastimes: faking returns, losing parts, and shortchanging customers.

Before unlocking the door, he set the cooler down at the trash can. Snatching the lid off the can, he grabbed up the bag and pulled it out. Walking around the side of the building to the dumpster, he set it down and rummaged through it for receipts. Lots of people threw them away as soon as soon as they walked out of the store.

Fortunately, no one had thrown in a coffee or yogurt yesterday. When the receipts weren't messy, this was the easiest extra money he could make. Faking a return and entering in the computer that he had shipped the part back allowed him to pull cash out of the till and take it home that day.

He looked for three things: an amount between ten and fifty dollars, a date within the last two days, and payment in cash. Four receipts fit the bill; a nice take, almost a Benjamin. Unlocking the store, he jammed the receipts in his front pocket and walked inside.

After disarming the alarm and taking the cooler to the break room, he went to the safe under the counter and spun the dial. He got it open and thumbed through the ones and fives to make sure he had change for the day. Once the drawer was in the register, he lifted the baseball cap off his head and ran fingers through his hair again.

Not much to work with yet today for the shortchanging. He rubbed the stubble on his jaw and looked down at the stubborn grease around his fingernails. That radiator he replaced for his cousin last night had been old and dirty. What had his best friend wanted?

Oh, yes. Headlamps. Looking up at the clock, Jack saw that he still had twenty minutes before he opened. Dave hadn't left any notes for him, and the store was already in good shape. He had time. Sauntering down the aisles behind the counter, he made his way to where the lights were. He had to pull out the receipts from the trash to find his scribbled note with the model number from his internet search. Lesser cons would have looked it up on the store's computer, but Jack didn't like leaving clues.

The lights were bigger than he liked, but if he took them one at a time he could fit them in his lunch cooler. Since he was already prepared for the shift, he grabbed the first and brought it to the back room. Lunch went on the table, the part went into the cooler, and Jack was ready to go to his car.

The camera covered the front of the store, so he propped open the back door and walked wide of the front walk. The Mustang was parked out of the camera shot on purpose. When he got there he opened the back door and put his prize under a blanket in the floorboard. Walking wide again on his return, he secured the back door and repacked his lunch.

Jack sat down in one of the chairs. The break room reflected his boss. Clean, organized, straight. Dave was one tense dude for an Indian. Oops. Native American. Sometimes to mess with him, Jack put his feet on the table and leaned back in a chair to rest his eyes after eating. Dave hated that. He also couldn't stand messes. Had he figured out that Jack was creating them intentionally? Nah. Too stiff to see past the tip of his nose.

Chuckling, Jack rubbed the sleep from his eyes and put his elbows on the table. Clasping his hands together, he rested his forehead on his knuckles. If someone came in, they would think he was praying. Actually, he was wishing he had called in sick.

Someone was knocking at the door. Annoyed, Jack opened his eyes and looked up at the clock. 8:10? Jerking awake, he scrambled toward the front. The last thing he needed was an angry customer telling his boss he had opened the store late. Rushing around the counter, he looked to see who was waiting and let out a sigh of relief. Krazy Knable was out there. Even if the old German were to tell, Dave wouldn't believe him.

Jack shook his head as he approached the man. Knable wore a white long sleeve dress shirt, discolored and yellow around the armpits. The cuffs were buttoned at the wrists, as always. Suspenders held up dark slacks that brushed the tops of his shiny white sneakers. His white hair was slicked back and so thin Jack could see the mottled skin of his scalp. Glasses perched on the end of his nose so he could use his long-range vision to look inside.

Turning the lock and opening the door, Jack made a mock bow. "Opening early just for you, Mr. Knable!"

After a pause, he looked up. Krazy Knable was staring straight ahead without blinking. Oh, this was going to be too easy. Holding the door open with his foot, Jack rubbed his hands together and smiled. He reached out and caught the old man's elbow and ushered him inside.

The routine was the same every time Knable came. He would walk in the store about five feet, stop and suddenly look around as if he had never seen the place before. Then he would turn to his right and go to the far aisle. After walking up and down every one, he would go to the counter and ask where they kept the spark plugs. After hearing they were behind the counter, he would inquire about plugs for a '69 Chevy Chevelle and buy a set. Then he would shuffle out to his new Buick and drive off.

Jack had never seen him drive a Chevelle.

Knowing he had some time, Jack looked out to make sure no one else was waiting. He hustled to the back room with the second headlight, put it in his cooler, ran it around the outside to his Mustang, and returned to the store.

He would tell Lance later they were sixty bucks apiece but he got them for fifty with his discount. One hundred dollars plus fifty for the install. Lance didn't have to know it was all profit. Served him right for the six invitations.

Back in the store, Knable rounded the last endcap and looked more bewildered, more anxious. His step had quickened a bit and he was muttering.

"Where are they? I have to have them. Where are they? I have to have them."

"Can I help you, sir?"

Knable turned around as if he had never seen Jack before. He blinked twice and went back to his search. Once again, Jack shook his head. Every week he did this. Why didn't he come straight to the counter? Why did he need a new set of spark plugs every week, for that matter? Knable got to the end of the last aisle, which was right in front of the cash register on the counter. He paused, pulled at the ends of his sleeves, ran a hand through his hair, and then carefully turned to approach.

"Excuse me, sir," Knable said. "Can you help me?"

Jack rolled his eyes. "I'll see what I can do, Mr. Knable. I'm pretty busy right now."

"Perhaps I should come back another time."

"No, no," Jack said. For some reason, Dave had a soft spot for this old guy. "Just tell me what you are looking for," and then, under his breath, "as if I don't already know."

"My wife is concerned about how our vehicle sounds and she wants me to perform a tune up on it. Where are your spark plugs?"

"You know the year, make, and model?" Then Jack mouthed the next words with Krazy Knable.

"It's a 1969 Chevrolet Chevelle, standard model, manual shift."

Jack put his elbow on the counter so he could look at the computer screen above the register. Using the mouse, he went through the menu. He could have said, *Those are R44XLS plugs. You need a whole set, right?* But that's not how the game was played. Mr. Knable would want to check the screen to make sure Jack was right.

"Here you go. R43s or R44s. Do you know the size of the engine?" Mr. Knable looked at the screen and then looked at Jack. "I will take a set."

"I've got four different kinds, running from ninety-nine cents apiece to about four dollars each."

"Nothing is too good for Mrs. Knable."

"Okay. With tax, that will be $33.81"

Jack turned to go get the ninety-nine-centers. When he came back, Krazy had two twenties sitting on the counter. Without ringing up the sale, Jack opened the cash register. He placed the one and the five in Knable's wrinkled, upturned palm and then sprayed the change over them.

As the old man turned to go, Jack pocketed the two twenties and shook his head. If there was a god, why didn't he take care of people like Krazy Knable? What kind of god would let Jack rip him off like that? No god Jack Ilsey was ever going to trust, that was for sure.

"In *God* we trust," Krazy Knable said.

Jack started. That was different. "What did you say?"

"In God we trust. God seems emphasized somehow."

Jack couldn't suppress the shudder. Was Knable an idiot savant? Could he read minds? *Well, maybe you can trust him, Krazy, but not me.*

"You can, too, Ilsey."

"What did you say?" Jack gripped the counter. He felt like the world had shifted.

Knable never turned around. His chin on his chest as if praying, he continued, "You can if you want to."

"I don't believe there is a god."

"I do!"

Krazy Knable put his change in his pocket and shuffled for the door.

Snatching his hat off his head, Jack tried to calm himself. He felt feverish, like someone had turned the heat on in the store. Did Knable know? Was he trying to tell Jack that he knew he was being conned? He set his cap on his head again, dry washing his hands. Bouncing on his toes, he watched the old German get to the door and pause. He couldn't take it anymore.

Rushing around the counter, Jack approached the man. "Hey, Mr. Knable, wait up!"

Looking up at Jack as he approached, Knable said, "Do you believe in god, young man?"

"Here, Mr. Knable, I almost forgot," Jack said, thrusting the two twenties into the wrinkled hands. "Dave told me not to charge you the next time you come in."

"Do you believe God can forgive anything?"

"I—I guess so."

"Even me?"

Jack stared at the man. Was this some kind of weird psychology? Was the crazy coot implicating him? One look in the old man's eyes told him the truth. Old Knable was worried about himself.

"Yes, Mr. Knable," Jack said. "Even you."

A tear escaped the old man's eye. He turned to Jack and put the twenties in his smooth, grease-stained hands. "You need this more than I do, young man. But you don't have to steal it from me anymore. Just ask me."

Long after Krazy Knable left, Jack was in the break room with the four receipts laid out on the table in front of him. He wasn't sure what to do anymore.

KLAUS

I must stop doing this.

The door is locked when I get there, which confuses me. The young man who works here, Jack, has his car parked in its usual spot. I don't have a watch, but it is Tuesday and I am here, so it must be after eight in the morning. I'm always here on Tuesday at ten after the hour. Papa taught me to be courteous to business owners and give them time to prepare to serve me.

I curl my hand into a fist and rap on the door with my knuckles. My knee hurts again this morning; rain may be coming. When there is no answer, I rap a little harder. I have to be careful, though. This old skin tears easier than it once did. I remember working on autos with Papa, changing out a transmission and catching my hand on a radiator fan. Sliced my left index finger to the bone. They stitched it and in two weeks the scar that now runs along that finger was all one could see of the wound. Nowadays, I can rub something wrong and have a nasty wound for a month.

Turning my fist sideways, I use the soft pinkie side of it to bang harder on the door. My stomach is churning a bit, and not from the yolkless egg I ate this morning. What will I do if they do not open? I know I do not need this, but I can't stop myself. Even if that young man overcharges me again.

Perhaps today is the day. If no one is here, I can't buy them. If I can't buy them, I will have to admit the truth to myself. If I admit to the truth . . .

No. No. I can't, and I know it.

I let my glasses fall to the tip of my nose so I can look through the glass door to the store inside. Where is he? I am lifting my fist again to risk a hard knock with my knuckles when Jack scurries out of the back room. He has a worried look on his face until he sees me and relaxes. Krazy Knable, he calls me, as if I didn't know. He has never asked me for my first name because David always calls me Mister Knable. David is a good man who indulges me quite a bit. Jack is a rascal. He smiles at me and bows as he opens the door.

"Opening early just for you, Mister Knable!"

He is late and David will have his hide for it. My brow is knit and my eyes are blazing, but Jack has bowed so low he doesn't see. He doesn't know the trouble he is in. Papa had a nickname for me when I was a young man. He called me *Lehrling Chirurgen*, Little Surgeon, for the way I could flay a man alive with my tongue. I decide to wait until I have my purchase to give him the lashing he deserves and step into the store.

I am overwhelmed. The store hasn't changed.

It's not one of those neat places they have now, where one can't tell if the employees have ever worked on a car. This is the gritty inside of a place where men of cars work. Grease and oil and dust lay in places they shouldn't. Packages of new parts don't look new because they have been hanging there a while. The owner gave up servicing cars long ago, but no amount of cleaning could make the place look different.

Standing there, I am transported. It's 1978 and I am entering the store because my wife has told me that our Chevelle is running rough. We haven't had the car for long, so I figure I need some spark plugs. A tune up and oil change goes a long way sometimes. I have everything I need to change the oil, but I need the plugs. Where would they keep them? Not wanting to bother the clerk unless I have to do so, I decide to walk through the aisles first. Papa said to be courteous to business owners when I can.

This all runs through my mind as if I am there, but I'm not. I'm right here. I know the plugs are behind the counter. I know I can get them for about five dollars, and I know I have spark plugs stacked along the wall of my garage at home. I have covered a wall with them, but I can't stop myself.

I turn right and head toward the aisle furthest from the counter. Running a weathered hand through my thinning hair, I touch things I may purchase down the road. Knuckles gnarled from holding wrenches and cracking them against engine blocks brush against a set of windshield wipers. The Chevelle will need them soon.

The Chevelle might need them, but I doubt it. I don't let myself think why yet. I never let myself think why until I get home.

I'm sorry, Maria! I should have bought the cheap ones. I should have made time.

Retreating into myself (I watch my mind go there sometimes, like a ghost at a haunted house watching little kids run from my "Boo!"), I walk the aisles looking for the spark plugs behind the counter. I am almost to the very end of the last aisle, to my great relief. I must stop doing this.

"Can I help you, sir?"

I turn and look up at Jack's sardonic eyes. I can't tell if he has watched me the whole time or if he is smug that he got so much done while I took my weekly trip around his store. I realize I have been muttering, and hear the last four words echo in my ears, ". . . have to have them."

No one calls me *Lehrling Chirurgen* anymore. They call me Krazy Knable.

Even knowing this, I turn back to finish my search. At the last endcap in front of the register, I stop. Despite the madness I can't manage, I know what Papa would want me to do. I pull at the ends of my sleeves, run a hand once more over my hair, and then carefully turn to approach.

"Excuse me, sir," I say. "Can you help me?"

Jack rolls his eyes. I am an old man, but I want to punch him. "I'll see what I can do, Mister Knable. I'm pretty busy right now."

Refusing to take the bait, to look around at the empty store, I reply, "Perhaps I should come back another time."

"No, no," Jack says. He knows I will come back when David is here and tell him Jack was too busy to serve me. David will know it for a lie. Jack is a rascal, but he is not stupid. "Just tell me what you are looking for," and then, under his breath, "as if I don't already know."

"My wife is concerned about how our vehicle sounds and she wants me to perform a tune up on it. Where are your spark plugs?"

"You know the year, make, and model?"

"It's a 1969 Chevrolet Chevelle, standard model, manual shift." I am not angered that Jack mouths the words as I say them. I am not frustrated. I am ashamed. I cannot help myself. Maria deserves this ritual. God deserves this ritual. My punishment is to revisit this store every week, perform this same transaction every week.

Jack puts his elbow on the counter so he can look at the computer screen above the register. The computer was not here in 1978. David installed it a year ago, and I am unsettled by it. I have used one before, but the computer does not fit my memory of that night. Jack doesn't see how his use of the mouse to go through the menu turns my stomach. He could have said, *Those are R44XLS plugs. You need a whole set, right?* But Jack came after the computer was installed, and now he has changed how the game is played. I am pulled a bit from my memory and look bewildered at the screen. Jack thinks I'm checking on him. I'm just trying not to remember.

"Here you go. R43s or R44s. Do you know the size of the engine?"

I glance at the screen and then at Jack. I know what I need to say, but it doesn't feel right anymore. Jack and the computer have changed everything. I take a deep breath and say, "I will take a set."

"I've got four different kinds, running from ninety-nine cents apiece to about four dollars each."

This very sequence is why I come every week. The prices were different in 1978, but the statement was much the same. I didn't want the cheapest kind. Maria deserved better.

"Nothing is too good for Mrs. Knable," I say, and I am transported back to when David's father ran the store. He had told me how much the plugs cost then and I didn't have the money. I could have bought the cheap ones, but I didn't. I told him I would see him on Friday when I got paid, but I forgot. That weekend, I went drinking with some buddies and spent the money.

Which is why the Chevelle wasn't fixed. Which is why it stalled.

Which is why the train . . .

"Okay. With tax, that will be $33.81."

Jack turns to go get the plugs, so he doesn't see the tears in my eyes. Pride and selfishness cost me my happiness all those years ago. Jack thinks I'm crazy, but I am not. I remember my daughter holding my hand while the doctor shared what it meant to have the onset of dementia. I remember the urge to go get the plugs I never bought. I remember the twisted wreckage and the closed casket, and for the first time in years, I don't want the plugs.

But I need them. I lay two twenty dollar bills on the counter so that I can't change my mind. Jack will give me cheap plugs instead and not even ring up the sale—four plugs can't cost over thirty dollars—but that is part of my penance. I killed my wife all those years ago, and no amount of logical explanation will let me forget it or forgive myself. My daughter forgives me, and I trust that. How can I trust that God would forgive me when one of His angels died because of me?

Jack sets the boxes on the counter and opens the cash register. He places the one and the five in my wrinkled, upturned palm and then sprays the change over them.

They don't quite cover up the back of the five, and I see something written on it there.

"In God we trust," I say. I hear Jack's voice but miss what he says. I am too focused on the underlining of God. What were the chances? How often have I had money in my hand? Never have I seen a bill marked like this, and I happen upon it now as I am asking these questions?

I realize Jack must have inquired about what I muttered, so I say, "In God we trust. God seems emphasized somehow."

Then I read what is written underneath. "You can, too, LC."

I shudder. LC. *Lehrling Chirurgen.* A fresh memory invades my routine. Papa is sitting on his favorite chair, squatting there like an old gnome in his dark living room. The television is on, turned down low. I am crying on the couch and Mama is holding me. Papa rubs his face and then waits until I can look him in the eye.

"You are not God, Lehrling Chirurgen," he says. "You cannot know everything. He knows everything, but you do not."
"Then why did He let me wait? Why did He not make me buy them?"

"He is a gentleman, son," He says. "He will not make you do anything."

"That gentleman let me kill my wife!"

"Enough!" For the first time in years, my father stands. "You are not God, Lehrling Chirurgen, and you cannot know everything. No one knows what happened tonight! You shame her memory and throw away your life out of self-pity. Life happens, son, and so does death. You must forgive yourself, and you must trust that God can forgive you."

"What did you say?" I turn to see Jack gripping the counter, the color drained from his face. Has he heard my thoughts? I hated Papa for what he said that night. I told him I could not trust God to do what He should not do.

Papa's reply had been the same as the next phrase on the back of that bill, so I read it out loud. "You can if you want to." I hear Jack respond, but I am caught up in my revelation. The looping hand of a young lady, so much like the writing of my Maria, finished beneath the other phrases, "I do!"

Maria? Is that you? After all these years, are you speaking to me? Do you trust God to forgive me? Do you forgive me?

I put my change in my pocket and shuffle for the door. When I reach it, I pause. Is it even possible? I consider Jack, dirtying his soul every day, stealing more than money; stealing his pride and replacing it with shame until he can't stand himself. Isn't that what I have done?

Rushing around the counter, Jack approaches me. "Hey, Mister Knable, wait up!"

I look up at him and say, "Do you believe in God, young man?"

"Here, Mister Knable, I almost forgot," Jack says, thrusting the two twenties into my hands. "Dave told me not to charge you the next time you come in."

I am not deterred. "Do you believe God can forgive anything?"

"I—I guess so."

"Even me?"

Jack stares at me. I see him searching my soul and I wonder if this is what it feels like for Jesus to look at me. He is testing me, asking me if I mean it. He sees that I do.

"Yes, Mister Knable," Jesus says. "Even you."

A tear escapes me. I turn with my tithe and press it into Jesus' smooth, grease-stained hands. I look up into his face. The illusion is gone and I see Jack again.

"You need this more than I do, young man. But you don't have to steal it from me anymore. Just ask me."

I open the door and walk out to my old Buick. I don't have a Chevelle anymore because my wife died in an accident years ago.

SETH

Hey, Dad. 6:25pm

What's Wrong? 6:29pm

Nothing. Why? 6:29pm

Seth Dawson kicked the front wheel of his bike so that it started rotating again. Birds were starting to sing, signaling that the day was escaping him. He would have to meet Blaise at Tess's house in a couple of hours. They didn't know the Graybills very well, but they knew Tess had always looked up to Blaise. In a way, they were using her desire to be friends to have a conversation their parents could know nothing about. Seth shook his head. If this was the right thing to do, why did they have to hide it?

The cell phone chirped at him and he looked down. The face of his father was looking up at him, the formal "Lance Dawson" showing up in white letters in front of the man. He was in a business suit, looking crisp at the breakfast table.

Seth had used that picture a year ago because breakfast was usually the only time he saw his dad. A financial advisor, "Lance Dawson" had worked sun up to sun down as long as Seth could remember; until six months ago. Seth picked up the phone and touched the screen to answer it.

"Because you never text me," his dad said.

"I text you."

A chuckle met his half-truth. "Yeah," Dad said, "But it's 'Dad, can I get this game?' or maybe 'Dad, can we order pizza tonight?' It's never something as simple as 'Hey, Dad.'"

"Yeah, I guess so." Seth looked down at the toes of his two-hundred-dollar sneakers. The bike tire had left a dark smear on the left one. His mother would freak and buy him new shoes, even though he didn't want them.

"Seth?"

"Yeah?"

"Want me to come to where you are?"

Oops. The very question he was most worried about. "No, dad, I'm . . . I'm at the park outside of town."

"On your bike?"

"Yeah."

"That's quite a ride." The ride was half an hour, which meant Seth wouldn't return in time to finish homework or chores; but then, he never intended to get back for either. He braced himself for the lecture. "Talk to me."

Maybe this new version of Dad is okay, after all. Seth took a moment to reposition himself on the picnic table. Anyone who thought Indiana was all flat cornfields had never been to the southern part of the state. Well, there was still corn; but this was his favorite place to come and think.

The trees offered good shade and the hill fell away from this table to a cliff separating the trees on the right and left. The result was a panoramic view of the last stretch of land to where the Ohio River snaked along. August now, so not the collage of colors that would mark fall. Still, it made Seth imagine Ireland with all the greens and browns showing up so vibrantly. This evening, the sun impressed an orange tint on the scene.

I'm stalling, Seth thought to himself. "Dad, you know how I've been saving up to get that new gaming console?"

"Yeah, I do, and I haven't changed my mind about helping with that."

"No, no," he said quickly. "I'm not asking for money, I promise."

A pause on the other end. "I'm sorry, son. That wasn't fair."

Who are you and what have you done with my father?

Seth couldn't say anything for a moment. The old Lance Dawson never apologized. He would have accused Seth of 'being untruthful' (Dad never said 'lying' since he was sometimes 'untruthful' to his clients to get a sale) and launched into a full-scale berating about how important integrity was and how necessary earning the money himself would be.

That was before he and Mom started attending Beulah Community Church. Before everything started changing. The wind kicked up, rattling the leaves above him and making a small flock of birds take flight. Seth watched them for a moment longer before answering.

"You know it's been really dry, right?"

"Yeah. I heard on the news the other day that we were officially in a drought."

"Well, it's been hard on the grass cutting business."

Lance's chuckle made him smile this time. "I bet," his dad said. "Have you thought of another way of making money?"

"I should have, but I didn't. Instead, I went over to Krazy . . . um, to Mister Knable's house to ask him if he could pay me up front for mowing his lawn next week."

Silence on the other end of the phone. Seth held his breath. This was like asking for a loan, and Dad didn't want him doing anything on credit. Not the way to do business or life, son, because you put yourself in bondage to the person you borrowed from.

"Krazy Knable?"

Seth's turn to chuckle. "Us kids call him that. Have you ever been to his house? In his garage, he's got an entire wall full of spark plugs."

"A what?"

"Yeah, a wall full of them. They're still in the boxes, stacked neatly. They cover an entire wall."

"Did you?"

"Did I what?"

"Did you ask him for the loan?"

Seth swallowed. "I wanted to, Dad. Walked up to the house and knocked on the door. He didn't answer."

"You know how I feel about loans, son."

"I do, but . . ."

"Hold on," Lance said. Seth could hear him give a muffled order from a drive-thru menu. He had never learned how to mute his cell phone.

While he waited, Seth looked up. To his right, just in front of the shelter house, a squirrel sat on a stump and gnawed on an acorn. Seth watched the animal, understanding how it felt to gnaw at something hard. "Okay, I'm back."

Sigh. "I knocked on the door again, still no answer. Then I heard something, so I went over to listen from the other side of the big garage door. I could hear him in there, crying his eyes out."

"Could you see inside? Was he hurt?"

"Not exactly. The sun was bright today, so I had to shield my eyes and press against the glass to look in there. Those spark plugs had tumbled all around him."

"What did you do?"

"I . . ." Seth started, felt a lump in his throat. He had almost turned away. Krazy Knable could have been seriously hurt, but all he could think about was running off and pretending he hadn't seen anything. An old man on the floor, God knew what happened to him, and Seth had turned to leave.

"Hold on, gotta pay," his dad said. Seth watched the squirrel, still working on that nut. He kicked his tire again. Another scuff. He decided to tell his mom he wanted to buy his own sneakers. That would get dad on his side and give him some time to break these in. "Okay, go on."

"I wanted to leave, Dad. But then I remembered how Jason helped that woman out on Sunday. Remember me telling you about that?"

"The waitress?"

"Yeah. I thought about that and thought Jason wouldn't leave an old man on the floor like that."

"You're right," his dad said. Seth could hear the smile over the phone. "Did you go in?"

"Yeah. The side door was unlocked, so I went inside to see if I could help him."

"Was he hurt very bad?"

"Not on his body," Seth replied.

"What do you mean?"

"Well, I went in and asked if he was okay. He kind of pushed the little boxes out of the way and sat up, then patted a place right next to him. I was scared, but I got the impression he just wanted to talk. So I went over and sat down next to him. You should hear the story he told me, Dad. I know now why he buys all those spark plugs. His wife died in a car accident a long time ago, and he always blamed himself for not fixing the car."

"Oh, wow," Lance said. "She had a car accident?"

"Train."

"Yikes."

Seth blinked back tears. "All these years we've called him Krazy Knable, Dad. All these years, and we never thought he might need to tell someone what happened to Mrs. Knable."

"Thank you," his Dad said.

"For what?"

"Oh, sorry. That was for the cashier. What happened next?"

Seth looked down and dug the money out of his pocket. Three twenties and a five-dollar bill. For a moment, he sat there, remembering.

'So, my young friend, you have come to see the Lehrling Chirurgen, the Little Surgeon, the Little Child of God, and not for a sad story, I bet.'

Seth squirmed a little. He knew he had done the right thing by listening to the story. He could plainly see on Mister Knable's face the healing that telling had given him. But he had come for the wrong reason. How could he ask for money now?

'I just came to see if your lawn needed mowing, sir.'

'Ah. You are making money for something important?'

'Yes, sir. But not that important, I guess. I can come back next week.'

'You need the money quickly, yes?'

Seth squirmed. He didn't need the money; she did. The sooner the better. Each passing week made her decision more difficult, and it hurt Seth to watch her make it all over again. Seth nodded, not able to trust himself to keep the truth from this gentleman.

Krazy Knable dug into his back pocket and pulled out his wallet. 'How much more money do you need?'

'Oh, sir, I couldn't take a loan. My dad wouldn't like it.'

'Then he is teaching you well. It is not a loan. Consider it payment for services already rendered. How much do you need?'

'Um, sixty-five dollars.'

Mister Knable pulled three twenties out of his wallet, then chuckled. 'Somehow, it is fitting that you should need a five-dollar bill. Do you believe in God, young Mister Dawson?'

'My dad does now, sir. I don't know what I believe.'

'Go inside and get me a pen from the kitchen table and bring it to me.'

Seth obeyed. When he came back, Mister Knable had the five-dollar bill out, using his wallet as a writing surface. As he accepted the pen, he smoothed out the bill. Seth could see that others had written on it already. When the old man was finished, he handed the five-dollar bill to the young man.

'I have always believed in God,' Mister Knable said, 'but I never thought He believed in me until I received this five-dollar bill. I am praying you have the same experience.'

Seth looked down at the back of the bill.

In <u>God</u> we trust.

You can too, LC.

You can if you want to.

I do!

Under all of that, Mister Knable had written, "And He believes in you."

"Seth?"

He started, realized his dad was still waiting for an answer. "He gave me the rest of the money I needed. He said it was for services rendered."

"Wow, buddy, that's great! You did a good thing and got a reward for it!"

"But, Dad, I didn't do a good thing. I wanted to run away."

"You didn't run away."

"I was scared to sit next to him."

"You did sit next to him."

"I couldn't wait for him to get done with his story. It was terrible. Miserable. I felt so sorry for him and I didn't know what to do to make it stop hurting him."

"You did something. You listened."

Seth sighed. "Yeah."

The line went dead. Seth could tell by the vacuum of sound. He looked down at his phone and saw the picture of his father, then the screen went dark. Before he could hit the redial, movement on his right caught his eye. He looked over and saw a Lexus turn into the parking lot, pull into a space, and park. The small, stout form of his father stepped out of the driver's side, two bags of food and a drink tray with two sodas in his hands. The tight, even line of his dark brown hair was exactly parallel to the wrinkles above his darker eyebrows. His thick mustache covered a wide mouth with what his mom called kissable lips. She swore between his lips, his smile, and his words, his mouth made their living for them.

Seth took a deep breath as he watched his dad climb the slope. When Lance Dawson looked up at his son, the smile lit up his face in a way Seth had never seen before. Carrying dinner, he found his way to the picnic table and, despite the expensive business suit, stepped onto the bench and sat on the table next to his boy.

"Hungry?"

Seth nodded and took one of the bags from his dad. They started unwrapping everything in silence. Lance handed him his drink and Seth took a long draw from the straw. When he set the cup down, he hesitated with the burger in both hands. He suddenly didn't feel like eating.

"Dad, that's twice now I've been involved in doing something good. Both times, I didn't want to do them. What's wrong with me?"

Lance turned and rubbed his son's back. "Nothing, boy. At least, nothing that isn't wrong with me."

"Yeah, but now you and Mister Knable found God, right? So it will come easier for you."

"I wish it did. I lied to another client today."

The admission was not as impressive as the fact his dad had used the word 'lied.' Seth couldn't speak for a minute. When he found his tongue, he said, "Dad, what's happening to us?"

For some reason, his dad found that humorous. He smiled. Chuckled. Started laughing. Before Seth knew it, he was laughing, too, though he didn't know why.

Finally, the older man wiped tears from his eyes and tried to settle down. "Buddy, we're the same people we've always been. We've helped people before, right?"

"Mm-hmm."

"We're good people, right?"

"Yes."

"It's not different, just better."

"How?"

"Because now, it seems God is putting those moments right in front of us, and making us aware when we don't live up to who we are. Can I tell you about something that happened to me today?"

"Sure."

"Jack Ilsey called me. Something happened to him this morning at the store. I don't have all the facts, but whatever happened made him ask about going to church with me this Sunday."

"Really? Wasn't he mad at you last night?"

Lance nodded, took a drink from his straw. "Sure was. Know what's insane? It somehow involved Krazy Knable and a five-dollar bill." When Seth's eyebrow raised, Lance laughed. "It's what us kids who are grown-ups call him."

"No, Dad, not that." Seth opened his hand and gave the five-dollar bill to his dad.

"What's this?"

"I think it's the same five-dollar bill."

Lance looked at it, smiled. "Wow." He reached into the inside pocket of his sports coat and pulled out his pen. He set the bill down on the surface of the picnic table. As Seth watched, his father wrote *'He is real.'*

"Dad? What if someone has asked you to do something good for them, but you don't know if it's good for them?"

"I guess I need more information than that, son."

"I . . . I can't give it to you."

"Then the only thing I know we can do is pray that you make the right decision."

Pulling Seth close to him, Lance Dawson prayed his son would make the right choice and thanked God for giving them chances to do good things. When he finished, he gave Seth back the money. They turned to their meals and ate at the park together in silence as the sun began to set. On a stump not far away, the squirrel finally cracked the nut.

TESS

Dear Diary…

Wow, this brings back memories. I haven't wrote those two words since I got into high school, I think. Let me look. OMG! It's been almost three years since the date of my last entry!

I took a minute to look back at what I wrote that day. I was a sixth grader, getting excited about the new school year and was drooling over this cool Freshman named Chet Pearce. I had just found out his family called him "Little Chet" because he was named after his grandpa or something, and that he had skipped a year when he was little because he was so smart. Like being one year younger than all the other freshies made him more likely to notice me. How immature did I have to be to think a Freshman would look at a middle school kid?

Now, I'm the Freshman. I guess that means Chet is a big Senior now. Wow, has he changed. He's got a ring in his lip, which is cool, but I hear he's big into drugs now. Maybe that's a rumor, but he LOOKS like he's big into drugs, you know?

Okay, Diary, you aren't real, so I'm going to stop talking to you like you are a person.

I'm just confused, is all. I can't understand some things that happened tonight. Maybe I can understand it and that's the problem. It's all about Blaise Dawson.

I can't explain why, but Blaise has always been a kind of hero to me. She's a year older, for one, and yet doesn't mind letting me hang out with her. She's GORGEOUS, of course. Her dad makes decent money and her mom does, too, so she dresses in all the best clothes. Her skin is always tanned, and even though she doesn't need makeup to look pretty (jealous!), she does and it always looks good. She was the only freshman on the varsity team for cross country and she cheers during basketball season. She makes great grades, and everybody likes her.

Until this year, I mean. Gosh, one mistake and people get crazy. She got pregnant. Nobody is like giving her any grief about it. They just don't treat her the same. It happened at the end of last school year, so when school started this week you could tell she was. I don't get to see her too often, except at cross county practice. I admit it, I joined partly because of her. I like to run, though, don't get me wrong. I just liked better the idea of being on the team with her.

Practices at the end of summer were weird enough, but she told me last week she was thinking about quitting the team. (Heartbroken!) I was honored that she would tell me about her struggle. I didn't offer much advice, but she thanked me for helping her make the decision. So when she told me today was the day she was going to tell the team, I invited her to come to my house after. I figured she'd say no, but she actually said okay.

Blaise Dawson at my house!

Okay, back to reality. I didn't notice how odd things got until I watched her tell the team about her decision. The coach looked constipated. I guess he was kissing his conference championship goodbye but trying to be supportive. He said the right stuff, but you could tell he was close to trying to talk her out of it. He even told her to let him know if she reconsidered, and that running was healthy for her condition.

Like she had a virus or a cold or something!

That was bad enough, but the girls...

I don't know which one snickered, but they all looked guilty. One of the seniors looked plain mad. I'm just a freshie, so I didn't say anything. But I thought someone would say something. I was so glad for her when her dad showed up to pick her up. She went over to talk to him about it, but then he pulled away and left. I'm glad. When I finished my run, she was waiting next to my mom's car, crying.

I went up and gave her a great big hug, then opened the door for her. When we got in the back seat, she told me one of the girls had said some hateful things about costing them a great season by . . . well, let's just say the girl thought she made some bad decisions last spring. Then we sat in the longest, most silent ride of my life. Even my mom didn't try to say anything.

We got to my house, had dinner with my mom and brother, got some junk food and drinks and went to my room. For a while, she just laid there on my bed. I tried to think of stuff to do, but it all seemed selfish.

Blaise, will you do my makeup? Blaise, will you play this game with me? Blaise, do you want to prank some guys? I don't know. I was thinking of the dumbest stuff but saying none of it, you know?

So I did the only thing I could think of. I curled up beside her on the bed. We were there for a long time. I somehow got up the nerve to ask her what it was like being pregnant. At first I thought I'd messed up, but it got her talking. Most of it was not too bad, but I had a feeling she was not telling me everything. Finally, she sat up, wiped her eyes and said, "I bet my makeup is a mess."

Like she wasn't still gorgeous, even after crying!

Somehow that led into her telling me she thought I was pretty (she's jealous of my skin?!) and asked to do a makeover on me. I would have normally been excited, but I just kinda nodded. I mean, she needed something to do to take her mind off stuff. Anyway, it worked a little. We did her makeup and mine, fixed our hair. She asked me about my brother Alex, but not like she was interested in him or anything.

He only interrupted us once, by the way. Popped his head in and told her to give it up, I was unfixable. Let me just say she won't be dating him any time soon.

I showed her some stuff I liked to do online after that, but she got real antsy. Kept looking at the window and watching the sun go down. I asked if she wanted to leave, but she said no. She asked me another question and I was talking again, but I don't think she was listening. The sun went down and I was about to ask her again if she wanted to go home when I found out why she was so anxious. Her twin brother knocked on my window.

Okay, just for a second here. Her brother knew which one was my window. I don't know if he looked in tonight or what, but that's a little creepy. Even if he is as gorgeous as his sister. Even if I would absolutely go to a Prom with him, or the movie, or wherever he wanted to go.

She opens the window a bit and he says to come outside. When she turns to look at me, I just nod. I went in the other room with her right behind and yelled to mom that we were going out on the porch for a little bit. Mom wanted to know when Blaise was going home. I told her in a little bit.

Outside, she thanked me and then stepped off the porch to talk to Seth.

Diary, I can only tell you. I listened. Okay, you're still not a real person, so I'm not betraying Blaise. But I have to tell what I heard to someone.

Seth and Blaise were about twenty feet into my yard. He looked up at me then down at her.

"Okay to trust her?"

I don't know the exact words from here. I only remember Blaise giving me this friendship look that I'll never forget and saying, "She's the only one I trust."

Then she asked me not to tell anyone what I might hear and to watch for my mom and dad.

Oh yeah, Dad came home by then from the auto parts store. Weird thing, he asked me what I thought about going to church this Sunday. I asked him if I had a choice and he said actually I did. I told him I'd think about it.

So back to Seth and Blaise.

I let them know I would watch for them and that they could trust me. Here's the basic idea of what happened.

Evidently, Blaise had asked Seth for help paying for something expensive. Somehow, he got the money for her. She kinda started crying again and asked if he would give it to her. He paused for a minute—like at least a whole sixty seconds, but it seemed like an hour. Then he hugged her and maybe he meant to whisper in her ear. Maybe I just leaned in farther, or maybe it was so silent in the neighborhood tonight that his voice carried. All I know is what I heard him say. It went something like this:

Blaise, you're my sister and I would do anything for you. I've been thinking about this and I want you to know I had some strange experiences this week that make me wonder if what you're doing is the right thing. Because if what you're doing is not the right thing, then it's not right for me to help you. I've asked you to talk to Mom and Dad, but you won't. So I'm asking if you will talk to someone (anyone!) first. Don't worry, I'm giving you the money, but I want you to look at this five-dollar bill when I do. It's special, and maybe it will help you decide for yourself what you should do.

Then he gave her this wad of money with one hand and the different bill with the other. He hugged her again, grabbed his bike, and drove away. Blaise watched him disappear, then came up to sit with me on our porch swing.

While we sat shoulder to shoulder, she smoothed out the money on her lap and looked at the back. I can't remember what all it said. Somebody underlined "In God We Trust", and then a bunch of people had written stuff under it about how real he is and that they believe in him.

Then, all the way across the bottom, Seth had written, "He forgives wrong and blesses right."

I asked Blaise what he was talking about. She said she thought he meant that it didn't matter what I decided, God loves her anyway. Then we cried together, and I made my own decision.

I'm going to church with dad this weekend and see if that's what God really thinks. I hope Blaise talks to someone first, because I'm starting to think I know what the money is for. Oh, Blaise. I can't imagine what you must be going through. I wonder if you have to believe in God to pray for someone.

RITA

The sun was up, but Rita was not. She'd had a bad morning. Her oldest son had shown up at her doorstep — again — at two in the morning, needing to crash. At least he learned not to bring friends when he did that to her. Then sirens woke her at four. Sounded like an ambulance, but she wasn't sure. The alarm clock went off at six, so here she was at a quarter after seven getting herself out of the car.

Oh, and the coffeemaker was broken.

Rita rubbed the sleep out of her ice blue eyes and put her keys in her purse. Why did she get such satisfaction from listing all the bad stuff? She checked her new hairstyle in the rear-view mirror. When her next-door neighbor, Dolores, suggested Rita go to her stylist, she was skeptical. Dolores knew what she was talking about, though. Her curls weren't tight anymore, almost wavy, but she liked it that way. Neat around the ears, auburn where grey had been but dark everywhere else, the cut and color made Rita feel professional. That girl could work magic with her hands.

Maybe she could pay for Dolores' next hair appointment as a thank you. The woman was on a fixed income and no doubt had little to spare. Trying on a smile, she turned away from the mirror and made herself open the car door. She turned sideways in the seat, gripped the side of the door and the steering wheel, adjusted herself, and then stood up into a beautiful sunrise.

Breathtaking. From the parking lot of the crisis pregnancy center, she was facing away from town. God had his paintbrushes out, for certain. Oranges, yellows, deep reds. Rita patted the back of her hair with a chocolate brown hand as she heard her daddy's voice in her mind. *Red sky in morning, sailor's warning.* Maybe it would rain tonight, maybe it wouldn't; but this morning God had brought her a sunrise, a smile, and her daddy's voice. The chuckle came easily, warm and infectious.

"Gonna need your help today, Father," she said. "Got much to do and no desire to do it."

Turning, she shut the car door and recognized too late she hadn't fetched her purse. She reached out and almost caught it before it latched, which was bad. The car door clicked, but it had not shut all the way. Now, the door was locked and the light was on inside. Rolling her eyes, she bumped the door twice with her hip until it closed completely.

"You locked already, so why do I care?" She grinned again and turned to look at the sunrise. "You knew I was gonna do that, didn't You?"

Mouthing a silent prayer, she went around to the passenger side, paused to say amen, and pulled on the handle. It opened up. That meant her son had taken the car before he woke her up, took it God knew where; but this morning, his bad choices became a blessing. Rita retrieved her purse and started to rummage for her keys so she could get the supplies from the trunk.

"Excuse me."

Rita jumped and turned, feeling a tweak in her knee. Next to her was a little blue sports car, an older model but well-maintained. Inside was a young, tanned girl — cheerleader if she ever saw one. Her mascara was beginning to smear a bit from the tears. She was still beautiful. Clutching her purse against her, Rita tried to breathe as she checked the car for anyone else.

The girl was alone. Rita looked up, then looked back down and her heart leapt into her throat. This young girl had come for the center, which wouldn't open for another hour. What was she going to do?

"You work at the center?"

"You could say that," Rita responded.

"Volunteer, whatever?"

"Mm-hmm. What is it, child?"

"I'm Blaise Dawson."

"Rita Pennyworth." Suddenly, Rita realized she still had a death grip on her purse. She made herself relax. "I'm sorry, honey. You gave me a fright."

"I'm sorry. I thought you saw me."

"Sure didn't. But I see you now." Awkward silence. "You here to talk to someone?"

Blaise nodded her head. "I—I promised my brother I would."

The sun broke over the trees, bathing the girl in ethereal, orange-gold light. Rita looked on her and loved her. She was so overcome, she couldn't speak for a moment. They shared an eternity and were almost friends. It had been the same with Lianne.

"The clinic doesn't open until half past eight, so I can't let you in until then."

"I figured," Blaise said, shifting in her seat, gripping her steering wheel. She reached for the key to turn the ignition.

Rita reached in and put her hand on the girl's arm. "Where you going?"

"Um," Blaise said, looking down at the contrast of their skin tones. A sniffle escaped her. "School."

"Already might be late," Rita said. "Might as well talk awhile, you know?"

The girl put her head down, thinking. Finally, she took the keys out and put them in her purse. Turning her head, she looked up. She didn't have to say a word. Stepping back, Rita gave her space to get out of her car, then waited until the girl closed the door before opening her own and slipping the purse inside. They both leaned back against their cars, prepared to wait the other out.

Rita lost the standoff. "You pregnant?" Blaise nodded. "You sure? We got tests in there to be sure. Would be the first thing they want to do."

"I've been to the doctor already." Blaise stood straighter and turned sideways to show the baby bump.

"How far along?"

"Seventeen weeks." Leaning against the car again, Blaise put an elbow in one hand and wiped below her eye with the other.

Math. That would be four months or so; past time to be thinking what she was thinking. Rita shook her head. "Your makeup is holding, child. Not planned."

Blaise shook her head. "One time."

"All it takes." They stood apart from each other, a teenage girl in trouble and a troubled woman in her fifties. They were about as different as they could be, except for one thing — they were both here. "First time?"

"Only time."

"True?"

Nod. Wipe. Look away from the sunset back toward town.

"Daddy live in town?" Rita's guess hit the mark. "He go to your school?"

Wipe. Look down. Nod.

"Does he know you here?"

Tears, real tears this time. Blaise shifted her eyes so that she could see Rita's face without looking up. The effect was devastating. Young boy would kill to see that look right there, would feel like even the sunrise wasn't all that pretty.

"What to do."

"I can't."

A wind kicked up and tugged at Rita's bangs. Here it was. Again. The moment when she knew she was in over her head. God loved this girl, loved that child. Rita prayed for her silently and waited. She prayed for herself and felt a deep desire to shut up.

The silence was deafening between them, but around them, the morning went on. People drove down the street behind Rita. Someone pulled into the parking lot of the convenience store next door. A young man got out and looked over. He'd seen this pretty young thing from the street and couldn't help a second look. Still, Rita waited.

"I had to quit running yesterday. I thought I could do it, you know? But I read some stuff about it and realized I won't be able to compete. I can run, sure; it's healthy for me and for it. But I can't run fast, and I can't let myself get all stressed out." A mournful chuckle escaped her and the hand went back to the elbow, the other hand to wipe the eyes. "Not like I'm already stressed."

She looked up at Rita through her eyelids again, but the older woman let herself stay settled and watched. Blaise started tapping her foot. She grabbed both elbows and pulled her arms in tight against her.

"Cheerleading is out this spring," she said. "It'll be here by then, I guess, but not until the season is half over." Then, with bitterness, "I guess Tess will inherit that part of my life, too."

The wind stirred. Rita said, "Who's Tess?"

The question made Blaise consider for a moment what she had just said. "A friend, I guess. She's a year younger than me and I guess tries to do everything I do. All the time. It's a little annoying."

"And a bit flattering?"

"I guess so. I hope she doesn't . . ."

Rita stepped forward and put a hand on the girl's shoulder. "If she does, that's her choice, baby. Don't you take that on yourself, too."

Nodding again, the girl turned to look back at the center so that Rita's hand fell away from her shoulder. She turned back and started tapping her foot again. Rita waited some more.

"So I guess if I don't make the right choice, God will hate me or something?"

The world turned upside down. In a blink, Rita was not herself. She was a teenage girl who had let her guard down one time — one time — and had let a boy go farther than she intended. Maybe she even wanted it, maybe she didn't realize until too late what it might mean. Maybe she was taught the lie that the greatest expression of love was to give herself physically to this young man. When she looks back on it now, does she regret it? Would she regret it if a child wasn't involved? How had this bright young girl let herself get into this situation? A strong breeze picked up an old plastic bag and whipped it through the space between their feet.

"That what you believe?"

"I don't know. It's only important because that's what my Dad thinks. He's been big into church for the last few months and now he wants us all to believe."

"Do you?"

Blaise toyed with her bangs. "I go to church with him. The music is okay. I like the preacher, I guess."

"Do you?"

Pulling her cell phone out of her pocket, Blaise looked at the time. Saw there were messages; one from Seth, one from Tess, one from her coach. She didn't look at the words, exactly, just the names.

While she was looking down, the picture of her dad popped up and she couldn't help herself. She laughed. He had fallen asleep with a bowl of popcorn sitting on his round tummy and she took the picture to remember how the bowl went up and down to the rhythm of his deep snores.

"Do you?"

Blaise looked up. "I do. Seth told me so on a five-dollar bill last night." She dug into her pocket as Rita watched, dumbfounded. A wad of bills came out, mostly twenties. Quite a bit of money there. Money enough, maybe, to make a choice. Rita prayed again as Blaise searched through them and pulled out the bill in question. When the girl offered it, Rita enveloped her small caramel hand in the warmth of her own dark hands before receiving it.

Abraham Lincoln looked up at Rita without winking. He stared stoically at her, refusing to give up the secrets he was hiding beneath him. She was starting to wonder what the girl was talking about when another gust of wind pulled the bill out of her hand and sent it tumbling. No way was she agile enough to catch it with her other hand. But she did. She looked up at Blaise, her eyes wide and her mouth wider in a hearty grin.

They both laughed. Blaise said, "Nice catch."

"Baby, I couldn't do that again in a thousand tries." Rita looked down. The bill had turned over, revealing handwritten notes on it. Someone had underlined God in the phrase "In God We Trust." The rest of the words were written by different people attesting to the goodness of God. At the very bottom, she saw the words in question.

He forgives wrong and blesses right.

"I don't see it."

"There," Blaise said, "At the bottom."

"Oh, I see where your brother wrote something. Had to be a teenage boy to think that counts as writing."

Blaise giggled again. "I tell him he should be a doctor."

"It's readable, though."

"Then you do see it."

"No, I don't. You said he told you God will hate you if you don't make the right choice. This doesn't say that." Blaise waited, staring intently as Rita searched for words. She closed her eyes for a moment and listened. A horn sounded down the way. Birds chirped. The leaves in a nearby line of trees rustled. Opening her eyes, she looked deeply into Blaise's. "If you went inside, there would be brochures and stuff to tell you. God isn't just interested in your baby. He's interested in you."

The girl pulled back and shook her head. Shuffled her feet; held her elbows.

"What you think? That God saw you do that one thing you don't want to talk about and decided to punish you? You think He looked down and thought Blaise Dawson doesn't get but one chance to show me she's a good person? You think He's up there right now laughing because you're in this situation? Look at me."

She didn't want to. But she did.

"God — loves — you."

"He has a funny way of showing it."

"He sent your brother, didn't He?"

"Yeah, to give me money for my abortion and then make me feel guilty about it."

"No, you doing that to yourself. God don't need to help."

A spark leapt into the girl's eyes. "He's leaving me no choice."

"He is? Or you are?"

"What kind of counselor are you? Are all your volunteers this pushy?"

Rita's laughter shocked Blaise out of her anger, not because it was unexpected but because it just wouldn't stop. Deep from the older woman's belly, joy spilled out all over the parking lot until the girl couldn't help herself. She giggled a bit, too.

"What? What's so funny? Rita? Why are you laughing at me?"

Wiping her eyes, Rita Pennyworth said, "Oh, honey, I'm not laughing at you. I'm laughing at me."

"Why?" "Because you think I'm one of the counselors."

"You—you're not a counselor?"

She laughed again. "I clean the offices every Wednesday morning."

Blaise started laughing herself, then. When they collected themselves, they were wiping a different kind of mascara smear from their eyes. Rita stepped forward, turned around, and leaned against her new charge's vehicle.

"I'm not hired, paid, or even trained to tell you all you need to hear, Miss Blaise. I'm probably the last person you need to ask these questions of. But here's what I think. I noticed two things about you since we started talking."

On impulse, Rita straightened and tenderly turned the girl's shoulders away from the sunrise. Blaise was putty in her hands, though she shot a curious glance over her shoulder. The older woman nodded forward.

"Look that way, what do you see?"

"Town."

"Your past. Your worries. Your regrets. Every time you look away from me, you look back there. Like, if you look back that way hard enough, you'll figure out what to do. Now look down, what do you see?"

"My feet." "Look harder."

"My knees?"

"Getting warmer."

"My —" her voice hitched. "My baby."

"Not it. Him. Or her. You see that child? Now, in a few months you gonna wish you could see your feet again." Blaise laughed. "But right now, and maybe even later, you need to do more looking. Now, turn around here."

Putting an arm around her, Rita turned Blaise so that they were both watching the sun break over the line of trees. The wind kicked up and a flock of robins broke from one of them into the brightening sky. They watched for a moment together in silence.

"Jesus is the Son of God, sure enough," Rita said. "And He rose so that we could see Him and believe the first part of your brother's message. God forgives us for our bad choices. He wants us to know how much He loves us and that His love will never change. We can look at Him and we don't have to look back anymore — to our past, our regrets, our worries. That is gone. Now, look down again. What do you see?"

"My baby."

"Yes. And?"

Blaise chuckled. "And my feet."

"That's right, baby. That's your present. Ooh, that's good; thank you, Jesus. Your situation but also your gift. Not only is your baby precious to Him, but you are precious to Him. No matter what you done. But He loves you so much He wants you to have as few worries and regrets as possible. So He wants to reach you somehow, teach you how to make right choices. Don't presume on that, child. It's a gift. But don't you ever let someone tell you God hates you. How you gonna believe a man who died for you hates you?"

Peeking out of the corner of her eye, the girl said, "You sure you're not a counselor?"

Rita grinned. "I'd like you to meet a young lady. One of my best friends. Her name is Lianne, and I watch her little girl. I think it would be good for you to hear her story."

"She's like me?"

"Mm-hmm. Had some difficult choices to make, too; and still does. She's working hard to make sure that baby of hers grows up and makes good choices. But you should let her tell you about it."

"I think I'd like that." Blaise checked her phone and Rita smiled. Kids these days looked at their phones the way old folks looked at their watches; more for comfort than for purpose. "Oh my goodness. I'm going to be so late."

"Put my number in there before you go so you can call me."

The two bent their heads as the older dictated and the younger entered the information. When she finished, Blaise threw her arms around her new friend and hugged her tightly. Rita was only too happy to return the embrace.

Tears led to sobs and then to real grief. Holding her young charge gently, she patted the girls back and whispered "There, there," over and over again. When she was spent, Blaise pulled back and mumbled how late she was and then got into her car. She had started it and was waving and backing away when Rita realized she still had the five-dollar bill.

"Keep it!" Blaise yelled out the window, then, "Or give it away!"

As the little blue car drove off, Rita looked down at the bill. She could use it to help Dolores get her hair done. Then again, she could afford to help Dolores herself.

"God, where You want Mister Lincoln to go next?"

The day was still. Shrugging her shoulders, Rita got her purse out of the car. She paused a moment to write a note to call Lianne and tell her about Blaise. When she had her supplies out of the trunk and was almost to the front door, she thought about that new young pastor over at Beulah Community. He probably needed it as much as anybody.

Behind her, a breeze blew through the trees as the sun continued to rise.

PRESTON

RING!

In the stillness of his office, the phone was intrusive, alarming. He looked down on his left. The readout showed an unknown number with the name "R. Pennyworth." Nobody he knew. He sighed and turned his attention back to the screen of his laptop. Did that count as breaking silence? He read an article last Saturday about the value of being still before God and dedicating a set time to be silent. What better way to ask for God's blessing on his sermon preparation and at the same time make him focus on it? After all, Sunday's coming.

RING!

No, a sigh didn't affect the spirit of his attempt. Silly to even contemplate, and off point. He couldn't answer the phone and keep his vow, though. Computer screen. Focus. Redirecting himself (again), he watched the cursor blink. It looked like a big capital letter "I", off and on, off and on.

Maybe he could use that as a beginning analogy.

How often did he try not to let himself be the most important person in his life, but the "I" kept blinking back on. That's not bad. So this would be a sermon about . . . what? Selfishness? Selflessness? He opened his mouth to say there was no "I" in team, then remembered there was an "I" in silence.

RING!

And an "I" in ring.

Sunday's coming. What to preach? An old-fashioned conversation about sin and how "I" find ways to interfere in my relationship with God? *That is a better feel. Lead it to the Gospel, since that's what church is all about.* He wanted to find a way to lead the people to understand the Good News of Jesus. No, that wasn't right, exactly. Almost everyone who would be there on Sunday knew the Good News of Jesus. They didn't need to understand it. They needed to take it seriously. What did it mean to take the Gospel seriously?

RING!

This would be easier if he had any idea what verses he would be using. Planning services in chunks was all the rage-- per year, per quarter, or at least by the month. How did other preachers do it? He was so caught up in all his other duties-- not to mention a part time job at the convenience store — that most Wednesdays he did exactly what he was doing right then. Was it worth worrying about? About fifteen people attended service on Sunday every week. The remaining people took turns attending every second or third week. He never had more than forty, never had the same crowd from one week to the next. If he started thinking in advance, what good would it do?

Preston looked at the phone. No more ring. The display showed that R. Pennyworth had given up and not left a message. What had the person wanted? Would the phone recall an unknown number to call back? After all, it was the most up-to-date piece of equipment in the whole church. Just six years old. The laptop was a little newer, but still had an old version of Windows on it that didn't get updates anymore. The internet was not much better than dial up. The sound board given to the church years ago only had eight channels, which was fine since no more than 150 people could squeeze together inside. Of course, they couldn't even do that since the pews were immoveable.

Preston found himself hoping for another *Ring!* to distract him from this line of thought.

I. I. I. I. I. I. I. I. I. I.

No escaping the little blinky cursor. Sunday's coming.

Standing up, Pastor Preston Wilson scratched his goatee and looked around his "office." He wasn't sure, but he thought what was currently used as the church office used to be the space for the senior pastor. After so many resignations, the congregation put their spiritual leader in the narrow closet on the left side of the stage. Only one door and no windows. It's mirror image was on the right side of the stage and used for storage. His desk was the best piece of furniture, but only because it hadn't been replaced. Seemingly made from a single piece of wood, the thing hulked in the corner and practically cut him off from the rest of the room. Behind him were bookcases partly filled with books from a defunct church library. They cleared three shelves for him when he arrived eight months ago. He had boxes of books in the garage of the parsonage that had no home.

I. I. I. I. I. I. I. I. I. I.

He closed his eyes against the cursor and took a deep breath. The room was getting to him. Maybe the blank screen was, too? He opened his eyes and looked at it again. Nothing came to mind. Sigh. Preston turned sideways so he could pass his desk without knocking off the picture of his graduation day. Past that, he weaved around the old file cabinet and pushed the door open to where he would preach his non-sermon in four days.

He stepped into a small square of space sunk down behind the stage, walked the three steps behind the piano, turned left and strode to the pulpit. The wood was scratched and stained but had an authentic, wild, spiritual look to it. Had it been bulky, it wouldn't have worked. Preston liked to walk around when he spoke and he wouldn't have had room. Thin, used, the right height, it was the only thing he liked in the sanctuary. The walls were cracked and dirty. The pews were stained and peeling. The computer desk that served as the sound booth was pressed wood with a green curtain across its back. The sanctuary looked unused.

Tick. Tick. Tick. Tick. Tick.

Preston looked at the old kitchen clock hanging on his right, letting the congregation know when he was about to wrap up. Was that ticking as loud on Sundays? Why had he never noticed it before? Despite his vow of silence, a snicker escaped him. He imagined his sermons differently than he ever had before.

And that's because Jesus Christ died and rose again!
Dramatic pause to let it sink in.
Tick. Tick. Tick. Tick. Tick.

Jason's guitar squatted on its stand on his side of the piano. That young man had been a true Godsend. He had a humble way of challenging the members to accept some of the new music he was introducing. Soon, Beulah Community would rush into the 1990's of Christian worship. Well, that wasn't fair. Jason loved the folksy worship songs of the last ten years. They just weren't what Preston expected when dreaming up his first ministry.

Tick. Tick. Tick. Tick. Tick.

Time was slipping away. He didn't have a sermon, didn't have any idea what he was doing, and didn't have any money. Beth wanted him to get his hair cut this week. She told him she couldn't stand seeing her husband standing at the pulpit looking like a wild homeless man. He hadn't had the courage to tell her they couldn't afford it, so he told her he was going for John the Baptist. She had rolled her eyes.

ring!

R. Pennyworth, no doubt. Preston looked out over the broken sanctuary, thought about the broken congregation, and discovered he was broken, too. What did he have to offer them? What did he have to offer God? Eight months into his first ministry at the ripe age of twenty-four, and he already felt defeated. How did God expect him to lead His church?

ring!

What is church, anyway?

Stepping down, he walked down the center aisle and turned toward the bathroom in the foyer on his right. The. One. Bathroom. He opened the door and went inside, closed the door to seal himself away from the gathering pressure.

Turning on the cold water at the sink, he splashed his face with it. He looked into the mirror and saw a bleary-eyed young man with a mop of brunette hair, a straggling goatee, and the weight of the world on his thin shoulders.

ring!

He almost told the reflection to get ahold of himself, then remembered the vow of silence. Instead, he looked hard into the smoky grey eyes and willed life into the youth looking back at him.

Bang! Bang! Bang! Bang!

Standing up straighter, Preston listened for a moment. That was the front door. He had locked it when he came in earlier that afternoon so no one would disturb him. His mentor, Pastor Ezra, had told him to protect his time for sermon prep. Lot of good it was doing him. Should he answer? No, because it required talking; and putting on a mask, pretending to be whole so the broken person outside could pour out some great tragedy. He gripped both sides of the sink and willed himself to stay where he was.

Bang! Bang! Bang! Bang!

What would Jesus do?

Putting his hand over his mouth, Preston suppressed a giggle. Of all the phrases that had circled around in his lifetime, that one got on his nerves the most. It was an impossibility. We are not Jesus. We can't do what He would do. We can't even come close. In a funeral home, we can't raise the dead. In a hospital, we can't heal the lame or make the blind see (well, he couldn't, anyway). We can't die for a sinful person to save them and we can't know the right thing to say every time. We can't teach as well as Him, treat friends as well as Him, or love our enemies the way He does.

Preston looked at the door. No more banging. No more ringing. No more interruptions. He was alone with the next question that lit up his brain like a wildfire.

What good is Jesus? And if no answer suffices, what good is the church?

He looked in the mirror again, but this time he saw a different person. A charlatan. A liar. A doubter. A cool looking young guy making money talking about something he didn't believe enough to figure out how to deliver one lousy sermon. Unable to stand his reflection any longer, Preston turned and escaped the bathroom. Out the glass front doors, he saw an older black woman put her phone in her purse as she slipped back into her car. He couldn't see into her window because of something taped to the outside of the church in just the right place to block his view.

As the lady pulled away, he marched up to the front door to look at the envelope taped to it. On the way, he felt his shoe strike something light. He looked down to see where the mail had dropped into the slot at the bottom of the door. Bending, he scooped up three envelopes, a circular, and a postcard. When he straightened again, he was eye to eye with the envelope she had left. In black ink, it read:

To: Pastor of Beulah CC
From: Rita P.

R. Pennyworth. She had been calling from the parking lot. She knew he was in here. Whatever was in that envelope was too important for her not to drop off.

Too curious by half, Preston reached up and unlocked the door. Pulling the envelope off the glass, he brought it inside and opened it to find a page from a steno notebook wrapped around a five-dollar bill.

Pastor,
You don't know me, and I don't know you. I'm not asking for anything. I was just challenged by a young lady to give away this five dollars and I thought maybe you could use it. Praying it blesses you.

Rita Pennyworth

Shaking his head, he looked at Abraham Lincoln for a moment and noticed she had written something along the border at the top. *Turn for a blessing.* Preston did.

In God We Trust.
You can too, LC.
You can if you want to.
I do!
And He believes in you!
He is real.
He forgives wrong and blesses right.

Preston stared at it for a long time.
This is what good Jesus is.
This is what the church is.
This.

The red of the postcard caught his eye and he shuffled it out from behind the other mail. An advertisement for a local hair salon. Men's styles for five dollars. Preston smiled. Turning, he ran back to the old copier in the church office, placed the bill on it, and made an image of the back of the bill. He lifted the lid to turn over the five, but on impulse, he pulled a pen out of his pocket and wrote along the front left side. After copying it, he pulled the bill out and stretched it so he could see the front. Pastor Preston Wilson read aloud what he had written there.

"Praise Jesus."

When he got back from getting his hair cut, he had a sermon to write.

NOTES

Notes for Sunday, August 30, 2015. Title not yet decided.

Trying something different today. I don't even know how to organize this, so I'm just going to type while I'm thinking about it. Some things from today:

1. The blinking cursor is an "I" – good analogy of how "I" keep putting myself at the focal point.
2. My own doubts and hurts. How transparent should I be? The members want me to be confident and have all the answers, but I'm just a kid trying to wear my dad's suit.
3. My questions. What good is Jesus? What is church? What does it mean to take the Gospel seriously? What would Jesus do?
4. The $5 and the coupon. Wow. That story just keeps going. Tell them something about the experience getting my hair cut, too. What did I do to offend that guy? It's a good thing Mary was there.

REMINDER: Exegesis = finding truth from the text.

Eisegesis = finding text for the truth.

"I so Jesus" (dumb joke) = finding text to prove *my own* truth.

Don't do the last one. It's likely to be false.

I can't let my desire to tell a truth make me read into a passage. Since I'm starting with a truth, I better be sure the text I'm using says it. So, first, what is the truth I'm telling?

The good of Jesus is . . .

The Gospel

The church

The result

So let's look at Pastor Ezra's way of approaching the process.

KNOW:

What we need to know about this is that Jesus is the answer. What's the question?

BE:

God is asking us to BE the CHURCH.

(We probably need to know what it means to be the church, then.)

LIVE:

How do we live out being the church considering what we now know?

*** God is interested in the BE, not just what I KNOW or how I LIVE! ***

If I start with Jesus:

John 16: talking to His disciples, tells them they will grieve and then have joy, talks about them being able to speak to the Father themselves, how they will begin to understand it all. (John 18:19-24... This would go well with above. Jesus talking during His sham of a trial and he says while being questioned by the high priest, "I have spoken openly to the world. I always taught in synagogues or at the temple, where all the Jews come together. I said nothing in secret. Why question me? Ask those who heard me. Surely they know what I said.")

Luke 4/Isaiah 61: the beginning of Jesus' ministry. I always loved this passage, but does it work as well as the John passage?

Mark 14: the prostitute that washes Jesus' head with perfume (contrast with the story where the prostitute washes his feet with her hair?).

Matt. 28: The Great Commission. Always a good Gospel message, talks about what the church is supposed to be and that Jesus will be with us always.

If I start with the church:

Acts 4:32-35. How all the believers were of one accord. How they shared everything and testified to the resurrection. (Kinda weird, maybe, but can I put in the story about the widow with the two coins putting in "all she had"?)

Colossians 1:3-6. Paul talking about this church, excited about what is happening.

If I start with the Gospel:

I should have put Matt 28 here, maybe.
Romans is always good. Funny. I thought I'd have a lot of passages here, but I can't separate the Jesus passages from the Gospel passages.
(Face plant. Duh.)

Really like the John passage, maybe the others can be supports. What is it teaching us?
(Eisegesis, not "I so Jesus!" What does the passage REALLY say?)
John 16:
17 Disciples ask, "What does he mean we won't see him any longer? Going to the Father?"
18 They kept asking. We don't understand what he's saying.
19 Jesus saw they wanted to ask, calls them out on it.
20 "I tell you the truth..." *(look up this Greek)*
20 "you will weep and mourn while the world rejoices. You will grieve..."
        IMPORTANT POINT: Grief happens!
20 "You will grieve, but your grief will turn to joy."
21 "A woman giving birth to a child has pain because her time has come;
21 "but when her baby is born she forgets the anguish
21 "because of her joy that a child is born into the world.
22 "So now with you: Now is your time of grief, but I will see you again and you will rejoice,
22 "and no one will take away your joy."

What does grief do to us? What is Jesus hinting at? I could look up some psychology, but I think it's obvious. Grief is going to cause them to doubt. What are they doubting? Jesus will be dead. Gone. Everything they built their lives around involves Jesus. When he dies, anyone not following him will be glad the troublemaker is gone. But they will be mourning, and they will have doubt. They will be asking the same questions I was asking. What good is Jesus?

IMPORTANT POINT: Grief causes doubt.

So what is Jesus saying? I could say they will have the "last laugh", but that has a connotation that we are one-upping those who didn't believe. I don't think we will be thinking about those who are not with us. I believe we will be thinking about the One who is with us. By the same token, when the world hears what Jesus is about to do, they might anticipate or guess it, but we now know it: the troublemaker didn't go away. He lives and He is still causing that trouble today! We can even draw a parallel with now: Jesus doesn't seem to be here, and others are mocking us, celebrating while we grieve that we have to wait to see if He does what He said He would do. But when He comes back, He will redeem all that time. As I wrote on that five-dollar bill, "Praise Jesus!"

IMPORTANT POINT: Jesus redeems grief and brings joy.

So we should expect the Son to rise. ☺ Cheesy, but true.

1. Grief happens
2. Grief brings doubt.
3. Jesus redeems grief and brings joy.
4. Expect the Son.

INTRO:

"I" want to be happy. I do all I can, sometimes I do things that I think will make me happy but instead make me regret.

NO. Might have to save the blinky cursor for another time. I'm scared, because I think God wants me to be completely transparent and admit my time of doubt. In a way, I'm wondering what I have to lose. It's less constructed and more real, more authentic. It also leads well into the conversation I want to have.

Duh. Tell the experience that led me to the sermon.

TENSION:

Gonna Andy Stanley this part. He talks about finding the tension that everyone feels in the situation, the thing that needs to be solved and the emotion it causes. What is God asking me to solve this week? How did I get to those questions? Why were they so important to me? What I struggled with was being able to see Jesus (and the church!) working. Haven't we all wondered where He is?

Wait a minute. Save the grief sermon for another time. Eisegesis, not "I so" Jesus. This passage isn't about grief. It's about knowing and trusting Jesus. We are not unique in our situation. The first disciples had to ask, "What good is Jesus?" and even more importantly, "What is church?" and man, did they ever have to ask, "What does it mean to take the Good News seriously?"

POINTS:

    1.

Not yet. I have to pray more. I think God is doing something special this Sunday. All because of some writing on a $5!

MARY

ERR IN GRACE:
What are you doing up so late? Or should I say early?

AT HIS FEET:
You should talk! It's 2:45am where you are, too!

ERR IN GRACE:
LOL. Yeah, I guess it is. I don't know why I'm
up, and I don't know why I decided to check
and see if you were.

AT HIS FEET:
Mm-hmm. I know you were checking out what all
those other girls were doing. How many messages
did you get this week?

ERR IN GRACE:
Ms. Parkinson, I've told you before that I'm
not that guy. I don't attract that kind of attention,
and I wouldn't know what to do if I did.

AT HIS FEET:
Again, how many?

ERR IN GRACE:
Three! Woohoo! Three girls want to talk
to me! Wait, YOU are talking to me, so
Mary makes four! Woohoo!

AT HIS FEET:
Jerk. I knew when I signed up for this dating site
it would be full of jerks.

ERR IN GRACE:
Seriously, Mary. Why are you up so late (early)?

AT HIS FEET:
I don't know if I should tell you.
It's pretty spiritual.

ERR IN GRACE:
Um, we're on a Christian dating site…

AT HIS FEET:
LOL. I know that, and I'm STILL not sure if I should
share it. I'm kinda starting to like you (me and those
other three girls), and I don't want to scare you off.

ERR IN GRACE:
Try me. At worst, it will make my decision easier.
I can narrow my options down to three!

ERR IN GRACE:
Maybe that was too far. Really, Mary, you are the
only one I'm messaging. I denied the others. I'm
kinda starting to like you, too.

ERR IN GRACE:
Don't disappear on me. Tell me.

ERR IN GRACE:
Mary Parkinson, I can see that you are still online
with me. That means you are sitting on your couch,
curled up with your laptop, your fingers hovering
 unless they are wiping the tear away and now
you're afraid you'll get your keyboard wet…

AT HIS FEET:
Are you watching me? 'Cause that was kind of scary.

ERR IN GRACE:
How long have we been chatting like this?
I'm just getting to know you.

AT HIS FEET:
I know, I was just kidding.

AT HIS FEET:
Okay, this might take a few posts to get it all in.
You know I'm a hairdresser, right?

ERR IN GRACE:
Stylist.

AT HIS FEET:
Whatever. I was working today with Matthew.
Have I told you about him? He's the guy who
loves to talk about the three no-no's: politics,
gossip, and religion.

ERR IN GRACE:
Oh, yeah. I remember we debated whether
gossip should be included in that mix.

AT HIS FEET:
As I remember, you lost that battle. Anyway,
guess who comes in with a coupon for a
haircut? My preacher, Pastor Preston.

AT HIS FEET:
Matthew insists that men like to have their hair
cut by men more than by women, so he jumped
in front of me to take him to his chair.

AT HIS FEET:
I was upset a little. This young man is helping me
understand my faith better. Since he came to our
church, he's been challenging us to love God and
love each other.

ERR IN GRACE:
It's not true.

AT HIS FEET:
What's not true?

ERR IN GRACE:
Most guys prefer to have their hair played
with by women. Added bonus to the
haircut procedure.

AT HIS FEET:
Oh, right! I can see that. Anyway, I wanted to bless
him by making his cut free. Lost out on that chance
when Matthew took him back. Anyway, Pastor
Preston mentions his coupon and Matthew says
they can settle that later, have a seat. Pastor sits
down and I suddenly realize it's a trap.

AT HIS FEET:
A Pastor. In Matthew's seat. I take the next client,
but I'm distracted. I'm trying to listen in on their
conversation.

ERR IN GRACE:
Eavesdropper.

AT HIS FEET:
Sure enough, Matthew asks him what he does for a
living and of course, he answers he is a pastor. I
glanced over and saw Matthew's eyes light up.
The perfect competitor! So he tells Preston he is
an atheist.

AT HIS FEET:
Quick as a wink, Preston says, "What does 'atheism'
mean to you?"

ERR IN GRACE:
Oh, I bet Matt was licking his chops!

AT HIS FEET:
Matthew says, "There's only one kind of atheist,
Pastor." And Preston responds, "So you have
decided you either hate God or hate what He
has done too much to believe in Him?"

AT HIS FEET:
Matthew says no, that's not what an atheist is. Preston
says well, that's what some atheists are because they
have told me so. If that's not you, then there are at least
two definitions of atheism. So what is your definition?

ERR IN GRACE:
Pastor 1, Matthew 0.

AT HIS FEET:
I thought so, too, but don't you know with Matthew
there's no winning that game? He didn't sit back
and think huh, I never thought of it that way. He
LEANED IN, got a little red in the face, and said
atheists were intelligent people who didn't need
a crutch to get through life and were willing to
face the reality that we are all so much mud.

AT HIS FEET:
At that point, the whole shop went still. You could
hear the clack of scissors and buzz of razors, but
no one was talking. I was holding my breath!

ERR IN GRACE:
What did he say?

AT HIS FEET:
Pastor smiled and said, "So you believe we were
all made from the earth."

ERR IN GRACE:
Ouch! I'm sure that made the guy angry!

AT HIS FEET:
Well, yeah, he said he didn't buy into that
"barbaric mythology" about man being
fashioned out of clay. Preston asked if he
believed in evolution, and of course,
Matthew said yes. Then Preston said, "So
you do believe man was made out of goo,
but you can't believe he was made of clay?"

ERR IN GRACE:
That's a great answer, but a little harsh.

AT HIS FEET:
My thought exactly! But then Preston says,
"Matthew, I didn't come to argue. I'm just
Trying to take the edge off your argument.
We aren't that far apart if you are willing to
talk about it."

AT HIS FEET:
The whole shop went silent. Not even a clipper
or a razor. Matthew cut the top of Preston's
hair, biting his lip the whole time. I couldn't
tell if he was thinking or getting angrier.

ERR IN GRACE:
Both.

AT HIS FEET:
I think you are right. He didn't say another word,
and the shop slowly took a breath and became
busy again. When Matthew finished, he
brushed the clippings from Pastor, took his
apron off him, and led him up front to the cash
register. Pastor gave him the coupon
and then gave him the five dollar bill.

ERR IN GRACE:
So why were you afraid to tell me this story?

AT HIS FEET:
Hold on, not done. I had to refill my coffee cup.

ERR IN GRACE:
YOUR COFFEE CUP!!? You do know it's
now 3:30 in the morning!

AT HIS FEET:
I'm addicted. It's sad. Anyway, I don't know if I
can sleep because I have a decision to make.

ERR IN GRACE:
k. Tell me the rest.

> AT HIS FEET:
> When they went up to the counter, I couldn't help
> myself. I followed them. So, I was the only person
> in the whole shop who understood why Matthew
> got so mad. He started cussing at the Pastor, like,
> really crazy, off the charts cussing. Pastor Preston
> said he was sorry, that's all the money he had.

> AT HIS FEET:
> Matthew threw the five dollar bill at him and
> shouted more obscenities. He told him he didn't
> want his money, to take it with him. Preston set
> it on the counter and said he was only trying
> to pay for services rendered.

ERR IN GRACE:
(raises hand) I, um, I don't get it. It was just five bucks, so
he could do without it, but why was he so angry?

> AT HIS FEET:
> I knew why he was angry. I could see the bill in
> Pastor Preston's hand. It was turned so the back
> was face up. There was some writing on it about
> believing in God.

ERR IN GRACE:
Oooooooooohhhhh. Wow. Do you think the
Pastor was trying to be not-so-subtle? After
all, their conversation wasn't very subtle.

> AT HIS FEET:
> I guess I can't answer that for sure, but I think the
> Pastor was just trying to pay his bill. My friend
> James Randolph is the deacon who counts the
> offering every week. I don't know how they are
> still paying the Pastor.

ERR IN GRACE:
Is he full time?

> AT HIS FEET:
> Well, he isn't paid full time. He works at a
> convenience store, too, but right now I think
> his wife is bringing home the bacon, so to
> speak. They need his income to keep a tight
> budget. Don't think they'd be okay without it.

> AT HIS FEET:
> But here's the weird thing. I had seen the $5 before.

ERR IN GRACE:
I've seen lots of $5.

> AT HIS FEET:
> This one is different.

ERR IN GRACE:
By the way, I admire your pastor.

AT HIS FEET:
Because he was crazy enough to come
to our dying little church?

ERR IN GRACE:
Your alive little church. Would you call
me a dying little man if I had cancer? No,
you'd call me a survivor and give me the
encouragement I need to battle my disease.

AT HIS FEET:
Ouch. True. Ouch. Okay, my surviving
little church.

ERR IN GRACE:
But yes, for coming to your dying little church.

AT HIS FEET:
Are you this witty in person?

ERR IN GRACE:
Not by half. I need plenty of time to think of what
I'm going to say in order to sound this witty.

AT HIS FEET:
Somehow I doubt that. Anyway. I was at church
this last Sunday and sitting next to Dolores.
Remember me talking about her?

ERR IN GRACE:
I do.

AT HIS FEET:
I saw her look at that five and put it in the plate.
She had written something on it, but I didn't
get a good enough glance to see what it said.

ERR IN GRACE:
So you're an eavesdropper and a snooper.
Next, I'm going to find out you are a
gossiping religious politician.

AT HIS FEET:
Dale Randall Thomas, you take that back.

ERR IN GRACE:
Wow. The MOM VOICE even works
from a CHAT BOX!

AT HIS FEET:
May I finish?

ERR IN GRACE:
No more interruptions, I promise.

AT HIS FEET:
I recognized Dolores' handwriting on the back.
She had underlined In God We Trust and
written, "You can too, LC." I think she was writing
to her great grandson. They call him Little Chet.

AT HIS FEET:
She put it in the plate, and here it showed
up at my salon. I don't know where else it
has been, but you can't imagine all the
things written on that bill!

AT HIS FEET:
You can if you want to.

AT HIS FEET:
I do!

AT HIS FEET:
And He believes in you.

AT HIS FEET:
He is real.

AT HIS FEET:
He forgives wrong and blesses right.

AT HIS FEET:
There was no more room to write on the back,
so people had written on the front! And I
suddenly got this image in my head of that $5
traveling all over Beulah to end up BACK
AT MY CHURCH in my Pastor's hands.

ERR IN GRACE:
That's . . . that's crazy, Mary. I mean,
what are the chances?

AT HIS FEET:
Evidently one in one.

ERR IN GRACE:
Touche, mon aimee.

AT HIS FEET:
Now here's the super crazy thing. I gave
Matthew five dollars from my tips and
took it home with me.

ERR IN GRACE:
Really? Can you scan it and send it to me?

AT HIS FEET:
Is that legal?

ERR IN GRACE:
As long as I don't try to buy something
with it!

AT HIS FEET:
Okay, I'll do that when we finish talking.

ERR IN GRACE:
So, you said you are up because you have
a decision to make.

AT HIS FEET:

Yeah, I do. You see, I think Little Chet
is supposed to have this five dollars. I
volunteer sometimes at a halfway house
across town and one of the women confided
in me that Little Chet knew her dealer.

ERR IN GRACE:

I'm guessing not a car dealer. Are you sure
it's safe?

AT HIS FEET:

I'm sure it's not safe. I think I know where I
could find him, but it might look like I'm trying
to make a "deal." And a girl has to be careful
showing up at an inappropriate time.

ERR IN GRACE:

Mary, I don't know. That's . . . unsafe.

AT HIS FEET:

Crazy, I know. Hence the coffee and the 3:00 chat
with a guy I'm getting to know on a dating
service. You're my safest confidant because you
don't know anyone to tell.

ERR IN GRACE:

I can be in Beulah tomorrow. We could
go together.

AT HIS FEET:
Aw, shucks. Are you saying our first date
would be a visit to a known drug dealer?

ERR IN GRACE:
If it keeps you safe, yes.

AT HIS FEET:
You know why I have this username, right?

ERR IN GRACE:
Because Mary chose to sit at the feet of Jesus.

AT HIS FEET:
Why did you choose yours?

ERR IN GRACE:
Because too many times I've seen the church
 so focused on their truth that they forget to
show grace.

AT HIS FEET:
This would be grace.

ERR IN GRACE:
Yeah. And crazy.

AT HIS FEET:
People thought my Rabbi was crazy.

ERR IN GRACE:
Please let me go with you?

AT HIS FEET:
I haven't decided I'm going.

ERR IN GRACE:
Yes you have.

ERR IN GRACE:
Mary?

ERR IN GRACE:
Mary?!?

ERR IN GRACE:
When you open this up later, because I know you will,
I just want you to know I'll be at Beulah Community
Church this Sunday. I am smitten by you.

MATTHEW

He was standing in front of that young pastor, waiting to get paid. They were in the shop. Everything looked normal except for the graffiti covering the walls, the counter, and the preacher's skin. He offered the bill and Matthew looked down at it. He didn't want to touch it because he instinctively knew it was alive.

"I can't accept this."

"You have to. You cut my hair and I owe you and God will hate me if I don't pay for it."

"No, you don't understand. I can't take it."

"You think I'm condemning myself for you?"

"Look, dude, just think of it as a donation."

"God doesn't want your handout," the preacher said.

He wadded the bill in his hand and threw it so hard Matthew didn't have time to avoid it. The thing hit him in the chest and he caught it as it fell. Immediately, he opened his hands to drop it. Too late. The ink of the writing all over the bill slid off and joined together to form a long stretch of wire. When the wire wrapped around his wrists and pressed into his skin, Matthew knew he was in trouble.

Pulling himself through the murky waters of sleep, he sucked in a breath and opened his eyes. The sheet was wet where it had covered his torso. Looking over to make sure

Bonnie was asleep, he took a deep breath and scanned the familiar things around their room. The old dresser his in-laws had given them when they were first married. The alarm clock he still had from when he was sixteen. The two prints hanging on the wall opposite the bed: self-portraits of Van Gogh and Ann Mary Newton representing him and Bonnie. She always joked he liked Van Gogh because they both only half-listened to people. He joked she liked Ann Newton because, like her, she was her father's daughter.

Bonnie wasn't amused. Her father was a drunk.

The door to the bathroom was wide open. Hagrid must have been drinking from the toilet again (quieter this time to keep from getting caught). That big mangy mutt started the annoying habit two weeks ago. Matthew stared at the opening, a dark maw except the light in the mirror straight across from him. Moonlight seeped in through the window and across the bed so that he could see his silhouette in that reflection. Maybe Hagrid was innocent. Maybe his dream had been real. The two statements had about the same odds of being true.

He swung his legs over the side of the bed and sat up, rubbing the back of his neck. Bracing himself on the nightstand in case his knee gave out again, Matthew went to the bathroom to relieve himself. He washed his hands and splashed some water on his face, then squinted into the mirror while drying off. The gel had all but disappeared, leaving his short red hair thick and disheveled. The moon was too bright and his neck was stiff. Groaning, he returned to the dresser to change t-shirts. Had the a/c kicked off? No. More likely Bonnie had turned it off.

Shuffling out of the bedroom into the hall, he went downstairs to check the thermostat. Pictures marched alongside him down the steps, family moments marking seven years of marriage and the progress of Lacey and Brianna. The girls were two years apart but were often mistaken for twins. Lacey, the oldest, was eight and starting the third grade. Brianna was all grown up now and going to what she called "Lacey's School."

"At Lacey's School today, I made a new friend. His name is Steven."

Matthew's grin succumbed to the rhythmic ache growing around his brain as he turned the corner and walked to the opposite wall of the living room. As he reached for the thermostat, he heard the air conditioning kick on. So it was on, just bad timing. Stumbling into the kitchen, he popped a couple of pain relievers to curb the growing drum beat rolling from the back of his neck to his temples.

Upstairs, down the hall, back in bed. Bonnie had already stretched out so that he had to move her arm to get in. He smiled and pushed her over. She nestled back into her own pillow. For a little while, he watched her sleep and stroked the dark strands off her forehead. Each time his mind touched on the dream, he redirected himself. How long had it been since he'd had a nightmare?

He was at the shop again. Mary Parkinson was sitting in his chair, letting him trim her bangs. When he moved from her left side to her right for a better angle, he had to ask the next person in line to move back a little. As he looked toward the person, he saw the preacher waiting there with the five-dollar bill in his hands. Behind him, a line of people waited for their turn. They snaked from his chair around the counter and out the door. Checking the parking lot

through the windows, he saw the line twist and turn like they were
boarding a theme park ride.

Every single person had that five-dollar bill in hand.

When he woke this time, consciousness rode waves of
pain. Not daring to open his eyes—even the moonlight would
be too much—he lay awake until Bonnie's alarm clock went
off. The incessant buzz danced gleefully with his headache, a
demonic partner tap dancing on his brain. Bonnie finally
stirred and slapped at the snooze button. Nine minutes later,
the dance resumed. The demon was swatted away again. Nine
minutes waiting in dread, unable to get up or speak to avoid
the coming onslaught.

The click of the alarm shutting off was a relief. He felt
her stretch and then turn toward him. She might have fallen to
sleep there, but he didn't think so. Ten years of living together
had taught her much about him.

"Is it very bad?"

Matthew nodded.

"Can you stay home today?"

He carefully shook his head.

"I'll make some coffee. It helps sometimes, right?"

He lay very still. She got up. He could hear her putting
on her slippers, felt the bed release her, heard her walk out of
the room. Heard heavy, fleet paws.

"Hagrid!"

Too late. The dog bounded onto the bed and went for
Matthew's face. He put his left forearm into Hagrid's chest
and then pushed him off the bed with his right hand. Even as
he hit the floor, the mutt was off and running before Bonnie
could grab him.

"Sorry, honey," Bonnie said. She closed the door behind her.

Cursing Hagrid and Bonnie, he lay in the ensuing silence and traced his headache back to its trigger. Last night was quiet. The drive home had been uneventful. Work?

Blasted coupon. Owen said he had to compete with the twelve-dollar chain salons, get people to try them out. The people who came for a cheap haircut never came back, though. All they did was clog up Matthew's schedule and make him work harder to earn a decent week. Five dollars? For a professional cut? And people like that almost never tipped.

The old man must be hiding some financial concerns. If Owen would make the leap and sell the shop to him, Matthew could make it worth something. Owen and Mary gave away too many charity cuts to keep the salon afloat. If he was the owner, Matthew's first step would be to limit charity cuts to five a month, then three, then one, then ban them. Twelve dollars was a reasonable charge for a bad haircut. Those who didn't want to pay for a professional cut had other avenues, and the chains always ran those stupid five-dollar specials.

He could smell coffee now. The aroma eased the pain somewhat. Why did caffeine do that for him? He was just glad it did. However he felt, he had to go in today for at least a little bit. The door opened and he listened to his wife's footsteps as she brought his coffee to the nightstand.

"When you can sit up, it's right here, Babe."

"Thanks, sweetheart."

"You sure you're going in? You made a lot of money yesterday."

"And miss a dozen five dollar specials?"

He could tell she was giggling behind her hand, trying not to be loud. With a normal headache, that would have helped. She squeezed his knee as she went to her closet and pulled out some clothes for the day. Every clack of the hangers went right through him. Lying still, he concentrated on the woody scent of the cup sitting near his head. Coffee. When Bonnie closed the bathroom door and started the shower, Matthew swung his legs around and sat up.

Holding the cup with both hands, he took a sip. Hot, fresh, delicious. The caffeine would take a while to make a difference, but the sense of peace began immediately. Could liquid be a comfort food? He smiled a little, but that hurt, too. Lack of sleep always made his migraines worse.

Sleeplessness caused by dreams. Dreams caused by all the little sayings on that five-dollar bill, the one brought in by the preacher who had made a valid point that Matthew didn't like. He replayed the moment, slowed it down, tried to think it through. Asked if he believed in evolution, Matthew had said yes. Then the pastor said something about being made from mud—the typical Bible mumbo jumbo. He'd met people like that before and usually, they were pretty easily handled. Made from mud? Really? How can something as organic as a human being come from something inorganic?

Except wasn't that the whole point of evolution? That no god was necessary because inorganic material, if left to itself for millions of years, would eventually spawn organic life? The odds of winning the lottery changed with every day, but wasn't it true that sometimes people won? If no one ever won the lottery, people would stop playing. Matthew felt confident that time was the factor needed for evolution to occur. The preacher's faith was so ingrained he never had a moment of doubt. One of Matthew's principles was to doubt everything. So when doubts occurred about religion, he was willing to address them.

What hadn't occurred until yesterday was someone helping him see the paradox in his position. He denied that people were made from mud like it said in the Bible, but he also believed people could be made from . . . what had the preacher called it? Goo? What was the difference?

Matthew tried to open his eyes, closed them again. He took another sip and sat there for a while. He didn't believe in God, but He did believe in the nobility of man. Lying, leaving his integrity in shreds, was a sin against himself. He had to be honest. His struggle came from his poor reaction to the preacher's money-turned-missionary-tract. The migraine came from that tension. He chuckled. His first crisis of faith and if there is a god, he or she gives him a headache the size of Indianapolis. No, Chicago. New York.

The bathroom door opened, alerting Matthew to how long he had been sitting there. He had to get up, had to go in. Mary had bought that bill from him and he needed it. He drank more coffee, waiting for his wife to stop banging into everything and go downstairs. When she was gone, he carried his coffee into the bathroom and turned on the shower. The hot water on the back of his neck was soothing, the caffeine cutting the pain a little. When he toweled off and dressed, though, the throbbing had increased again.

"You be careful driving, Mister," Bonnie whispered, kissing him on the temple. He nodded and winced when she shut the front door. Grabbing his keys, he went out to his truck and drove to the shop.

Mary was parked near the road, early as always. Pulling up to the front of the shop, Matthew got out and let himself in. Every step marked time with the pulse of pain, but he pushed himself to walk toward the break room. He stopped when he heard voices. Owen was in there with Mary.

"Thanks, boss," Mary said.

"Know what you're going to do?" Silence. Mary was nodding, because Owen continued, "I thought so. Mary, you know how dangerous it is."

"I do."

"Is that five dollars worth your reputation? Your life?"

"No, but the message it gives is."

Matthew shook his head, immediately regretting it. He made a rash decision and walked into the room. The two occupants went silent, leaving a vacuum. They looked at him and saw the squinty eyes, the pale skin, the sheen of sweat on his forehead. Both their faces drew down into what he supposed were expressions of pity.

"Yes, I have a migraine; no, I don't need your sympathy."

Mary's face went blank, either honoring his request or offended by his bluntness. She turned and squeezed Owen's elbow, then walked out of the room. When the two men were alone, they stared awkwardly at each other.

"Matthew, go home," Owen said. "I'll take your appointments today."

"Don't you have your own?"

"No, I just came in because Mary called me."

"Mmm. She's going to do something crazy, isn't she?"

Owen laughed. "Matthew, we don't always see eye to eye; but I admire your straightforwardness. Yes, she's doing something crazy."

"Can you stop her?"

"I don't think so."

Matthew grabbed the bridge of his nose, closed his eyes. "I'm not big on taking favors, Owen. But I can't even think straight. Are you sure you can stay today?"

"You bet."

"Okay. I'm going to the bathroom and then I'm going home."

Owen patted his shoulder. "Good. I'll go get set up."

When the door to the break room closed, Matthew opened his eyes. He was alone. Glancing around, he saw Mary's purse in a cubbyhole on the far wall. Rushing to it, he pulled out her wallet and rifled through it. Not there. Opening the mouth of the purse wider, he pushed around the contents but couldn't find it. How much time did he have? Could he empty it on the table and put it all back together so she wouldn't know? Maybe on a normal day, but not today. He returned it and closed his eyes again. Where could it be?

Opening his eyes, he saw the corner of a bill sticking out of a pocket on the side. He lifted the flap and pulled on the corner. There it was. Turning to make sure he was still alone, Matthew pulled the troublesome money out of her purse and strode to the back door of the shop. Out in the alley, he looked around to see if anyone was watching. Too late for school children and day shift adults, too early for everyone else.

He was alone.

The dumpster was five steps from the door. A quick toss, a return to the break room, out the door, in his truck, and

Matthew was driving home. Despite the pain, he smiled. Knowing how much he would pay for it, he rolled down his window to stick out his head and shout at the top of his lungs.

"Let's see what You can do with that!"

The migraine lasted three days.

EVERYMAN

I am not different. I had a mom and a dad and two sisters; one older and one younger. We grew up together across the river from a mid-size Midwestern city. Doesn't matter where. Could be St. Louis, or Louisville, or Memphis. Dad was a carpenter and Mom stayed at home until Dad left. When she started working, Big Sister took care of us. She fed us and made sure we got to school. I was the one always making her fuss at me. I regret that sometimes, smile about it sometimes. We were kids. What did I know?

I am not mean, though. Never took out my issues with Dad on kids at my school. Didn't get into trouble just to get attention. My problems were mine; even growing up without someone to show me how to be a man, my mom taught me responsibility by getting a third job to keep us together. So I gutted it out in my classes and did my homework as long as Big Sis got on me. Turns out I was pretty good at two things: learning stuff and playing baseball.

I am not dumb. Watching the Cubs on WGN spoke to me about millions of dollars for playing a silly game. So many of them played baseball in college. Mom wanted me to go to college. I studied hard and practiced hard. My coach started me my freshman year at right field. Then second base. Then he let me pitch.

A state college took interest in me. My mom never liked baseball much, but she loved the idea of me getting a degree. Whatever it took to get into college, she bent over backwards with her schedule and our finances to let me play.

I am not lazy. I didn't go to one of the better colleges for baseball, but I did get to go to school at a place that turned out good teachers. I figured if I worked hard and made my own breaks, I could still get an opportunity. Big Sis was waiting tables, Little Sis was finishing high school. I wanted them both to have the opportunity I had. If I even made it onto a Triple-A club, I could pay for both. What I wouldn't give for that?

I am not just a jock. My advisor asked me once why I hadn't applied to some of the more prestigious schools. Money, I replied. Money. She thought I was smart enough to be an engineer or run for public office. I don't know about that. Good grades were easy to come by, though. Learning was the one thing that had never changed in my life, so I was always ready to dive into the next thing. Math, science, literature, whatever it was. A degree became a reality to me.

I am not uncultured. While in college, I discovered the arts and realized I had a knack for drawing and painting. Not only that, for some reason teaching those things was simple. If a classmate was struggling, I seemed to understand why and helped them improve. Already majoring in education, I wondered if teaching art was something I could do. My advisor helped me get into it as a minor and told me I should focus on teaching English as my major. Baseball was going to be my ticket out, but this teaching art and English thing was starting to make sense, too.

I am not selfish. During the off-season, I found out a local charity sponsored art classes for under-privileged kids. Admittedly, I did it so I could teach art. Once I started, though, I found out my heart was there all along. Kids from fifth to eighth grade came to the center and I helped them dream about art the way I dreamed about baseball. As I was pouring into the kids, they were pouring into me. Through those two years, I discovered my place — teaching art and English to middle school kids.

I am not unlucky. I don't believe in luck. My high school coach told me if I worked hard and kept my eyes open and took opportunities when they presented, luck would have little to do with my success. My life had shown me the truth of his words. Until my elbow injury. Until I couldn't pitch anymore. Until my dream died. For a while, I couldn't figure it out. How could God give me this gift of a slider, curve, and moving fastball and then take it away? I was angry, but I could do nothing about it. For the rest of the season, I did rehab to try to get back. I never played my senior year.

I am not full of self-pity. Despite my humble beginnings, I had been given a gift. I graduated with honors and was placed in a middle school in the northern part of the state. Though I had done some traveling while playing ball, never had I been so cut off from my family. Big Sis got married and divorced in a year, strapped with a child (that's how *she* put it). Little Sis went to a technical college to start a nursing career. Mom got to experience two college kids, a wedding, and a grandchild before she died.

I am not angry. I could be, but how can I judge what Dad did? He felt responsible for us after she died. He let Big Sis move in with him. Introduced her to heroin. I had been teaching for three years and was ready to give her money for college, but it was too late. She overdosed in my father's bath tub. He split. He always does.

I am not irreligious. I believe a God watches over us. I believe Big Sis and Mom are reunited. I don't know how it works, but I'm pretty sure it does; especially for people like those two. They never got any breaks. How can they be held responsible for that? Dad? Well, I don't know what's going to happen to him. I'm still trying to figure that out. The ones I'm worried about, though? Me and Little Sis. We had all the breaks. Have we done enough with them?

I am not cursed. At least I don't think I am. But when the school needed to trim the budget, art went first. And since they could also cut down on the number of English teachers, I was let go. Not much warning, no severance to speak of, just let go.

So I started looking for a job and found out one of the area schools back home was looking for a baseball coach. They brought me in and let me watch over study halls and teach one English class if I turned their program around. The first year we only won three games. The second year we sniffed at a .500 season. Ten games into the third year we had only won two. They terminated my contract.

I am not indifferent. I know what I need to do and I have the degree, the smarts, the drive, and the belief to make something of my life. I'm working hard and I'm keeping my eyes open, but opportunities are few and far between.

Little Sis moved to Oregon with her new husband, a doctor who takes care of her and their two kids. She's living like a queen there, and I could go to her. But they have a life of their own and I have never been a part of it.

I am not too proud. I've taken construction jobs, fast food jobs, odd jobs. I've stood out with the immigrants hoping to get a day of pay. I want to be someone, but I've been living this way for ten years and I don't know if I will get the chance to do life like everyone else.

I am homeless. Despite all my breaks, I find myself digging in this dumpster, hoping for some food, hoping to catch a break. I've let Mom down. I've let God down. I've let myself down. If only God would give me some sign that there is still a chance for me. If someone would just give me a chance to be who He meant me to be. I'll screw it up, maybe, but that's up to me. Just . . . just give me a chance.

I am surprised when my hand closes on something that feels like money. It's a five-dollar bill. I pull it out and brush it off, look at it. Money for food. I turn it over and see some writing on it.

In God We Trust.
You can, too, LC.
You can if you want to.
I do.
And He believes in you.
He forgives wrong and blesses right.

I turn it over and see more writing on the front.

Praise Jesus.
Turn for a blessing.

I am not a drunk or an addict. On my way toward town where I can fill my pockets with food that travels, I see a sign for Beulah Community Church. There's a beat up old car in the parking lot. I almost stop but decide against it.

I am dirty. All over. Inside and out. Who would want to see me there? I go to the Buck Apiece store anyway, suffer the stares and snide comments, the withering looks and amused faces. I get food and pay for it with money from God.

SPIRIT

HERE does not exist. Here is a description of a physical space wherein certain things are or are not. Here is where Dale is, approaching Dresser Avenue and Fremont Street three blocks south of the busiest part of Beulah, Indiana. Here means something to Dale. He is *here*, but not *there*, where he wants to be.

"Seriously?"

Dale wants to be *there*, at a hotel he found on his phone before it stopped working. Now he only knows he is looking for Jackson Street, which remains elusive as he sits at a stop light. He is *here*. I am here as well, but I am not just here. I am also there, and everywhere between. I am *present*, which is different than *here*.

Because I am *present*, I know where Dale is, where he wants to go, where he needs to go, and where he will go trying to get *there*. I am not surprised when he goes straight. I am *present* there as well.

Dale looks in his rearview mirror as if the answer is there. It is not. All he sees are the green eyes and tired face of a man who has spent half a day of his mortal existence in the vehicle he drives. His age is not important because time is not important.

I am *present* with him here as I am *present* with Elisha telling his servant to open his eyes to the Army of God. I am eternal, outside of time (what is time, but a countdown toward death?), and to be *present* is to see the span of the existence of the Father's children as a *moment*. This *moment*, I am *present* with Dale as I am present with the man he will meet as I am present with the woman he seeks as I am present with the pastor he will support and encourage as I am present with each of the people who gather to hear this pastor tell of the Son of the Father, the One Who sends Me.

I am not waiting to influence Dale as he drives two more blocks and on a whim — a nudge from me — turns left toward the store where he will stop. I am *present* in him, so I am in the moment as he weighs his decision and I press gently upon his will to choose left. He listens to me. As a Son of My Father, he often — but not always — does.

Dale rubs his eyes, fighting to stay awake. For him, death drags him toward his mortal end, wearing him down especially because he has denied himself the Father's gift of rest. He is worried about the woman since he discovered her intention. I have always known her intention, always known how the Father would protect her.

I am *present* with her as she rifles once more through her purse on her couch in her living room, looking for the gift that is not hers to give. I am *present* with the gift and the man who holds it so tightly in his hand, walking through the store, trying to find food, trying to avoid contact with others.

Unable to spot his *there*, Dale sees the store. He does not know what to do next because he needs the Father's rest. He is not *present*, he has transported himself to *there* in his mind and realizes he will need some things. I do not make him stop. I allow him the choice. He drives into the parking lot and parks his car. He is getting out as she is dropping her head into her hands as the Pastor is scribbling a few more notes as the wandering man picks up granola bars.

Time is nothing. Timing is everything. Inside the universe with the children of the Father, timing serves eternity while time chips away at it. I am the Master of *present* and I have chosen this *moment* for life to unfold again, as it always does, at the feet of the Son and the intention of the Father. Dale walks to the front door as the wanderer approaches the cash register as the woman cries out to the Father as the Pastor cries out to the Father, also. I am *present* with them all, with more than them, because time is nothing.

All over creation, timing is bringing man and man, man and woman, woman and woman together in an intricate dance and I am *present* with each one. For some, I am the One who presses them gently into an admission of guilt. For some, I am the One who provides jarring consequence to arouse conscience in the face of pride, selfishness, cruelty, waywardness.

155

For some, I am the One spurring them out of indifference, boredom, hopelessness. For some, I am the One who embraces them in their losses, their pain, their trauma. For some, I am the One who lifts their hearts to celebration, worship, praise. I mandate nothing, but I govern all. I am the Breath of Heaven, the Wind of God, the Presence of the Son. I am not *here* or *there*, I am not *when*. I am *present* in the *moment*.

Dale enters the store as the wanderer is paying. He is not aware of the significance. I do not make him aware. In the third aisle, he finds food, sustenance for his mortal body. He finds drink that is more for taste than for purpose. He gathers what he thinks he needs and carries it to the front of the store. His transaction is for less than fifteen dollars and he happens to have a twenty in his wallet. He gets back a couple of ones and the gift. He does not look at the gift. The timing must be right. He walks out of the store toward his car as the Pastor wipes his tears and writes the sentence I whisper to him as the woman says 'Amen' as the wanderer stops at the corner of the building to put his purchases in his pockets and throw his bag in the trash.

At his car, Dale stops to put the gift in his wallet. I am laughing, I am worshiping, I am exalting the Son as His name is praised, as the Father is validated, as I am working in the heart of My temple to bring about salvation, discovery, and growth. I am *present*.

He couldn't believe his eyes.

"No way." Dale Thomas looked at the face of Abraham Lincoln, could see the shadow of writing on the other side. In the corner was written *Praise Jesus* and at the top was written *Turn for a blessing*.

His hands shaking, Dale turned over the five-dollar bill.

You can, too, LC.

You can if you want to.

I do!

He is real!

And He believes in you!

The rest were on there, too. This was it. During the whole trip from his home in Mobile, Alabama, he had wondered if he would be too late. Mary was obsessed with giving her friend's gift to this Little Chet. If she did, would he have spent it on something at the Buck Apiece store? Was this proof that she already did the transaction or proof that she had decided not to go through with it?

A whisper in his mind, half an idea that made him lean back against his old, beat up Ford Escort and think. If she had already met this LC, he could do nothing about it. If she had not, he could either take it to her and make her let him go with her or get rid of it so that she never got the chance. Which idea was best? He didn't want to start a relationship with her by fighting, but he didn't want her to be in jeopardy. A sigh escaped him.

"What am I doing?"

You're going bonkers for a girl, is what you're doing.

Dale chuckled. True, very true.

The sun was bright, strong despite the late hour. He could already feel a trickle of sweat down the middle of his back under his T-shirt. Pale legs were roasting beneath the hem of his navy-blue golf shorts. Somehow, he had to find that hotel and get a room. Nine hours of driving, a few hours of sleep in his car, the stress of the situation made him all too aware of his own stench. He needed a good shower, a little sleep, and a chance to recharge his phone so he could find Mary's house.

He realized he was staring at the man standing by the corner of the building. Despite the heat, the man wore an old army jacket and blue jeans. A wanderer. A homeless man. Dale blinked the sweat out of his eyes and locked gazes with the man. He didn't think. Rarely had this happened, but he was in the *moment, present* with the man. He watched as his companion grimaced and looked down at his shoes. Dale pushed away from the car and walked toward the other gentleman.

"My name is Dale," he said as he extended his hand. The fellow took it, but half-heartedly and without response. "Can you do me a favor?"

Surprised, the man looked up. "Sure."

"I am lost. I'm trying to find the Motel 6, but my phone is dead and I can't seem to locate Jackson Street. Can you tell me where it is?"

The man smiled. "You're about two blocks south of it now."

"Can you show me?"

"You can't find your way two blocks north?"

Dale chuckled. "Okay, you got me. Let me be honest. I just drove here from Mobile, Alabama, and I stink. I need to get a shower and some sleep because tonight I'm going to meet my future wife. I hate it that I've had to go more than a day without that sleep or shower because it makes me feel grimy and frustrated. When I'm grimy and frustrated, I think everyone else knows it."

The man looked away for a moment, then looked back. "You feel like an unpublished novel."

Something caught in Dale's throat. He stood there, trying to get words to come out. They wouldn't come. The two men stared at each other, understanding each other, realizing neither would ever know the depth of the other's loneliness. No tears. No words. No reason for either.

"I have no ulterior motive," Dale finally said. "I'm offering you the other bed, use of the shower, and a chance to tell me your story if you want. When you want to go, you can go. I don't have anything valuable with me, so I'm not going to watch you like a hawk. You'll have a key and a place to stay for the next three days."

"Conditions?"

"You let me tell you my story. You go to Beulah Community Church with me on Sunday. You let me pay for stuff."

"Why?"

"Because sometimes I feel like an unpublished novel, too."

The man stared at his benefactor for five, ten, twenty, thirty seconds. "Thank you."

"It's nothing."

"It's everything. It's timing."

"Let me start with this."

For the second time that day, God gave a homeless man a Lincoln.

DALE

Sleep eluded him despite the exhausting day. Rubbing his bearded chin, Dale turned the rub into a scratch, the scratch into a two-handed scrubbing of his entire face. He wanted to take another shower, but he didn't want to wake the other occupant of the room. He still didn't know the man's name.

What am I doing? This isn't me.

The Dale of yesterday wouldn't have offered to share a room with a stranger for three days. Of course, the Dale of two days ago wouldn't have driven from Alabama to Indiana for anything short of a family emergency. A soft chuckle escaped him. The Dale of last year would never get involved in an online dating service, either. Maybe this made more sense than he was willing to admit.

This Dale is new.

New Dale stood in front of a hotel window in a white T-shirt and grey boxers, a pair of ankle-high socks covering his long toes. Years had been kind to him, but he was no longer able to play much full court basketball. Too much sitting on the job without a plan for exercise.

Still, he was quick around the bases for his church softball team despite the extra twenty pounds he carried. For a moment, he let himself see the silhouette of his frame in the reflection of the window. Would Mary find him attractive?

Insane. Mary. She was eight years his junior, a pretty woman who hadn't spent much time on romantic relationships. He remembered browsing the online information for the matches from the dating service. Hers was the only one without a picture. He almost passed it by—his first mental image was a mousy older woman afraid of her own appearance—but he changed his mind when he read her introduction.

> *Hello! My name is Mary Parkinson and I am a hair stylist in the Midwest. I have a great circle of friends, a wonderful boss, a nice home, and a loving church. I feel blessed by God every day and have everything I need except someone who will share it. What matters most to you?*

Old Dale read it over twice and ticked off what the paragraph told him. A self-made woman, a career woman, an independent woman, a spiritual woman, looking for someone interested in commitment. None of this separated her from what the others said about themselves. But the question . . .

Behind him, a cough escaped the homeless man sharing his room. He turned to watch as the man wiped his mouth, turned toward him from his back, and settled back into slumber. His hair was still wet from the shower he had taken. They spent the evening eating at a family restaurant, dropping by the Goodwill to get a fresh outfit and Wal-Mart to get underclothes. He hadn't talked much. When New Dale asked him his name, he responded, "Everyman."

The most intimate thing he learned about the man was when they watched a little bit of the Cubs/Dodgers game on ESPN. Baseball was more than a hobby for this man. He knew too much about the process. No way he played pro ball and ended up where he was, right? But he knew when the manager was going to call the bullpen before the commentators did. He got lost in it for a while and talked about the dugouts at Great American Ballpark in Cincinnati. Was he a batboy?

New Dale sat on the back of the chair behind him and tried to make out if the man's eyes were open. He had admitted he was yet to turn forty, so they were of an age with each other. What had this man seen? What had brought him to this place? What right did he have to ask? After all, here he was sharing the same room hours north of his home, and for what?

No. For whom.

Old Dale had looked at Mary Parkinson's question and knew he was facing a watershed moment. The cursor was blinking in the reply field before he knew he planned to answer. What mattered to him? His career as a banker? His ministry to the teenagers at his church? Those were not bad things to list. Were they accurate? Could he be more predictable? Should he spiritualize it? He could put his relationship with God, his relationships with people. Should he personalize it? He could say his search for the right woman or, even subtler, his search for a woman who knows what matters. Maybe that wasn't so subtle.

Minutes later, he typed, *I'm intrigued by your question because the truth is I don't know.*

What followed was an almost nightly conversation about what was important, how having a partner helped or hindered it, and if they could be the partner the other needed. He had never had those conversations with anyone. Naturally, he fell in love.

After three months, she finally shared a few pictures of herself. He couldn't believe she wasn't already married. He couldn't believe she found him attractive. He couldn't believe she might one day be his. They discussed meeting one another right before their late-night conversation about the five-dollar bill.

How crazy, that he drove all that way, got lost in town, and ended up at a store where that money ended up in his hand? Old Dale wouldn't have made the trip. New Dale didn't know what to make of the coincidence. He needed a New New Dale to make sense of this turn of events.

The thought brought another soft chuckle from him.

"Can't sleep?"

Startled, Dale looked again at the face of Everyman. "I guess not."

"My fault?"

"No," Dale said. "You aren't snoring and you don't scare me." "What is it, then?" This, too, was a watershed moment. This new question was as potent as Mary's first. Where Old Dale had wanted to jump into an answer at first, New Dale let himself stew in the process. Silence stretched comfortably between them until Everyman appeared to have returned to sleep. Dale lowered his head for a moment, raised it to meet the man's intent stare.

"I am unworthy of two things," Dale said. "God's grace and this woman's love."

Everyman shifted, pulled the covers back, sat up. He rubbed his face and pulled his long, damp hair back. "You don't think helping out a homeless man qualifies you for both?"

"No," Dale said. "I'm not helping you in the hope that God will like me."

"Aren't you? That's why most people help a person like me."

"You think that?"

Everyman laughed. "I know that."

Dale thought about it. Who knew better the state of morality in America than a homeless man dependent upon the good will of others? Is that why people were good? Wait. That's not what the man was saying. He might believe people would do good things for selfless reasons. He doesn't believe people will do good things *for him* for selfless reasons.

"You mean most of us use you as a moral lightning rod. We spend most of our time not noticing you. So when we do, it's either out of a sudden sense of guilt or a recently exposed sense of selfishness."

"I'm rooming with a philosopher," Everyman said. Dale couldn't control the laughter that spilled out of him. Everyman joined him and at the end was lying back across the bed, holding his stomach. Dale left the window and went over to his own bed. Sitting down, he felt the weight of everything. Everyman raised his chin so he could look up at Dale and said, "You are a good man, Dale."

"Am I?"

"Yes. I have turned down offers like yours before."

Dale smirked. "Why would you do that?"

"Because," Everyman responded, "most of the offers come with strings, or expectations, or at least a confession of my life. You pressed for none of those. Dale, you are the real thing."

After a time, both men crawled beneath blankets and went to sleep. Dale never admitted his desire to steal the five-dollar bill back from a homeless man. Everyman never admitted his desire to give the five-dollar bill back to his new friend.

The most important exchange had not included Lincoln.

HOPE

Table 12 was kind of cute. He had a rugged air about him, like he had seen things she couldn't imagine. Someone recently cut his dishwater blonde hair, but she thought he might be more handsome with it wild. His eyes were blue, but not piercing. Too much thousand-yard-stare in them, like he was looking through the world instead of at the world.

Hope often said psychologists would die to learn what servers learned about people. She knew much about them in the first thirty seconds by what they said and didn't say, how they looked or didn't look, what they showed was important. Did they notice her name tag because they were interested in her name? Or was it just hanging in a convenient position on her body? Did they include her in the conversation, or expect her to pass by like a ghost to make sure their needs were met? Did he let his wife order first and talk to his kids? Did she disappear into her phone the moment she put her menu down?

Standing in the station, waiting for the new pot of coffee to brew, Hope bit a fingernail and looked at Table 12 again. He had ordered the buffet for his Friday lunch and stayed at the table through her whole shift. He ate deliberately and drank coffee and water in equal measure. Earlier when he had gone to the bathroom, he had waited until she walked by to let her know so she wouldn't clear his table. They were the only words he had spoken since he had used her name and said hello before ordering.

"He's cute, isn't he?"

Hope started, making Theresa laugh. She turned to her friend and saw the dancing eyes and furtive smile. "Stop it right now, Terry Berry."

"You are blushing."

"I'm trying to figure him out."

Theresa filled a glass with ice and stuck it under the Diet Coke. "Mm-hm."

Shaking her head, Hope dragged the pot of coffee out and filled a new cup for Table 12. Theresa always teased her about guys who sat in her section, but she was the one who always got dates with them. The shoulder length blonde hair crowned her head in tight curls and she had a way of lighting up the room with her laugh. She was thinner, prettier, and funnier than Hope; but she was also needier, less sure of herself, scared of being alone.

Stop it! Sometimes Hope couldn't turn it off. "Really," she said, "he just doesn't fit anywhere."

"Girl, you gotta get a degree in that."

"What?"

"Psychology." Theresa put the Diet Coke on her tray and pushed another ice-filled glass under the Dr. Pepper. "I look over and I see a mysterious, good-looking man with strong hands and a thoughtful smile. You see a human puzzle."

As she set the second drink on her tray and grabbed an extra set of rolled silverware, she wrinkled her nose at Hope. Patting her friend on the rump, she grabbed her tray, shook her head, and sashayed over to the couple at Table 3. Hope watched her go, saw the two look up from their menus and smile at her. She leaned against the counter for a moment and bit her nail again. As she did, the rough edge of the Velcro on her wrist brace grazed her chin.

She looked down at it. Hauling heavy trays of food around for the last six years were taking their toll. The doctor had suggested she give that wrist a break, but servers didn't make money when they took time off. The black wrap was a symbol of her pretty cage. She barely made enough to survive but made too much money serving tables to stop and do something else. Even if she went back to school, how would she afford it?

When she looked back up, Table 12 was watching her. This time, she could feel the heat rising in her cheeks. Grabbing the tray, she made her way toward him, refusing to be the first to break eye contact. He never looked down. She smiled as she got closer and carefully swung the tray from her shoulder to her waist to set the coffee cup down. Collecting the half-empty cup already on the table, she checked the level of water in his glass. When she was sure of the tray's balance, she turned toward Table 11 where a family of four had finally left.

"Miss?"

Hope stopped and turned back to him. "You need something else, sir?" He opened his mouth to say something, then shook his head. "I appreciate the coffee."

"You are welcome." "I'm going to the bathroom again." "Your coffee will be waiting for you."

He smiled sheepishly. "Thanks."

As she cleared the plates from 11, she watched Table 12 extricate himself from his seat. He turned back to the table and pulled the fresh cup under his nose. Eyes closed, he breathed deeply and took a sip of the hot black liquid.

"My grandma got me started on this stuff when I was four," he said.

She laughed. "I can't imagine liking coffee that young."

"Oh, she doused it with cream and sugar to take away the bitter edge. I drank it that way until I started my first teaching job."

"Yeah," Hope replied. "A lot of my long-time coffee addicts drink it black."

"That's because they've burned off their taste buds." She laughed again and he chuckled. "Excuse me."

She nodded at him as he turned toward the restrooms, then watched him as he walked away. A teacher. Somehow that didn't fit him. His measured gait was strong, confident despite his sense of social insecurity. If she had to guess, he was an athlete in high school. He carried himself like a jock. It didn't make sense. How could a handsome, fit man like him get so lost?

Tossing silverware onto the used plates, she set the half-full glasses around the edges of the tray until she knew it balanced well. Hope walked through the swinging doors and set the dirty dishes in line for the dishwasher. She looked around the kitchen for Theresa, but she wasn't there. No doubt smoking out back. Grabbing the empty tray, she walked both of their areas to look for unneeded dishes and unmet needs.

Theresa met her back at the hostess desk. No new customers were coming in, but that wasn't a surprise. The lunch rush was over and the dinner rush was still two hours away. Fridays were always long because they usually worked a double. The best money of the week was made today.

"Thanks for clearing my table," Theresa said. "When do you want to take a break?"

They usually ate from the buffet mid-afternoon so they didn't have to leave the building. Hope looked out the front door into the parking lot. Rain had started, which was bad for business.

"I guess now is as good a time as any."

"You should ask to sit with him."

"What?"

Theresa grinned. "Table 12. I bet he's waiting for the rain to stop before he leaves."

"Stop it, Ter," Hope said. "I can't go sit with a strange man like that."

"Well, I can," she replied. Hope looked up quickly and Theresa giggled. "That's what I thought."

Hope blushed again. "He's cute, okay?"

"And mysterious. We covered that."

"A human puzzle."

Theresa knit her brow. "I tell you what. Get you a plate and a drink, go sit at 13, but facing him. See what happens."

Looking over her shoulder, she saw Table 12 heading back to his seat. He stopped and looked out the window at the rain. For a moment, she wondered if he was going to leave. He picked up his coffee and took another sip. As he set the cup down, he looked around the room. Finally, he let his shoulders droop and sat back into the booth.

"Okay."

Theresa's eyes lit up. "Really?"

Hope didn't respond. She walked into the kitchen to tell Zach she was taking a break. He smiled and nodded and gave her permission to eat in the dining room. Thanking him, she turned toward the double doors and froze. Was she going to do this? Fighting inertia, she stepped back into the dining room and turned left toward the restrooms. Inside, she washed her hands and splashed some water on her face. She didn't have her purse, but she tried to manage the wisps of chestnut hair that had escaped her ponytail.

When she had done what she could, she stopped long enough to look at her reflection. What she saw surprised her. "I'm not so bad."

Her image smiled at her before she turned and went back out to corral a plate and a Sprite. She filled the plate with salad, topped it with the vinaigrette, and tried to keep her hands from shaking as she slid into the booth at Table 13. When she sat down, she realized she had forgotten silverware.

"You left an extra set here," Table 12 said. Hope looked up into his eyes and he smiled. He pointed at the roll of silverware on his table.

"Thanks," she said. She started to get up, but he waved her off and grabbed the set. He stood and took two steps toward her, bending to reach her table so that he was at eye level and as far from her as possible. Others might have taken it for a dismissal, but Hope understood what he was doing. He was used to people not wanting his presence and he didn't want to assume the right to be in her space.

She let him retreat. Wrapping her tiny hand around the napkin, she pulled it to her and unrolled the fork, knife, and spoon. Hope tucked the napkin in her lap and then bent her head over her meal. She thanked God for it and asked Him to bless her night shift, then grabbed her fork and started eating. On her third bite, she dared to look up at him.

"How did you do it?"

"Wha--? Oh," she said. Looking at her wrist to avoid his eyes, she continued, "I guess most people don't think about how hard serving tables can be on your wrists."

"Carpal tunnel?"

"Maybe," she said.

He smiled, but the gesture couldn't pull the wistfulness from his eyes. "But you can't miss a day."

"Nope. I can't."

"So you've figured out how to wear this food all through lunch and then eat it for dinner?"

Coming from someone else, she might have taken offense. Coming from him, it seemed like insight; like getting to know her. The heat in her cheeks pulled her eyes down to her plate. Had she met her match? He was quite the psychologist himself.

"I work doubles on Friday," she said around a mouthful of salad, then stopped and put a hand over her lips. "I'm sorry, that's rude."

"It's okay. You got to take a meal when you can get it."

When she looked at him, he was staring out the window at the rain. She said, "Are you waiting for it to stop?"

He nodded, then turned back to her. "I hope I'm not . . ." He chuckled. "I'm trying to figure out how to ask you to sit with me without using your name in the sentence."

Hope smiled. "Can I be honest?"

"I hope so."

They both laughed. He sat back in defeat and she covered her face to keep him from seeing how her eyes watered. Why was she so nervous? Before she could talk herself out of it, she grabbed her things and moved into the booth opposite him at Table 12.

When she felt collected, she looked up. "I was hoping you would ask me."

"Why?" Great. That wasn't the question she expected. Actually, she wasn't expecting a question at all. She wasn't as pretty as Terry Berry, but she knew she was attractive. Did this guy want her to admit she was interested in him? It didn't fit him. Wait, *was* she interested in him? Well, yes; but not the way he thought. Hadn't he said he wanted her to be honest?

"Can I be honest?" He smiled and said nothing. She took a sip of Sprite. "I can't figure you out."

He laughed. "That is not what I was expecting."

"Yes, it was," she said. It cut his chuckle short, caused him to cock an eyebrow. "You're used to people not knowing what to think of you."

Table 12 looked down into his coffee cup, played with the handle. Left-handed. Now that she was close and permitted to see him, she noticed the nicks from shaving and his cracked lips. His fingernails were a bit dirty and scars covered the back of his hands.

"Please," he said, pointing to her food, "eat."

"I'm sorry," she said.

"Don't be. I just know you don't have a lot of time and you need to eat."

She took a bite for him. He used the handle of his coffee cup to turn it in circles as he waited for her to chew. Silence stretched, uncomfortable, tense, but not awkwardly so.

"Do you always pray before you eat?" When she nodded, he asked, "Why?"

She swallowed and took a sip of Sprite. "I don't know. My mom would be disappointed if I didn't."

"You don't believe in God?" "I do, but . . ." She searched for an explanation. "I know He's there, but I don't know how much He notices me."

"How could anyone not notice you?"

She brightened, but when she looked up at him he was looking down. His face had darkened and now his eyes were the ones watering. She laughed. "That's the first line you've used in a long time."

He smiled. "Yeah, I'm really, really out of practice."

For a while, they sat in quiet. She ate carefully, making sure she didn't end up with dressing on her face or lettuce in her teeth. When she finished, she told him she wanted some soup and went to the bar to get it. Truthfully, she was surprised when he was still there on her return. She grabbed her spoon but sat back in the booth.

"What's your name?"

"Everyman," he replied.

"That isn't fair," she answered. He looked up. "I can't hide my name from you."

His eyes strayed to her name tag; then, recognizing where he was forced to stare, he looked away. Her heart leaped. She hadn't realized how tense she was until some of the wariness leaked out of her.

"I'm afraid if I tell you my name, I won't be able to stop." When she arched an eyebrow, he frowned. "Christopher. My name was Christopher Nash."

"Was?"

"Yes. Before I became Everyman, they called me Chris."

An hour later, Zach walked up to the buffet line and waited until he got Hope's attention. He pointed down at his watch until she understood. Time to get back to work. She didn't want to work. This man who so casually entered her life was most likely about to disappear. She might never see him again.

"You have to go, don't you?"

"I'm afraid I do. Does it help if I tell you I am afraid?"

"Why?" His favorite question.

"Because Chris will disappear and Everyman will walk out of here."

"It's the way of the world."

"It isn't. It's the way of your world so far."

"Nothing changes that."

She sighed. "Why did you invite me to your table?"

In answer, he reached into his back pocket and pulled out some money. He counted it until he knew it covered his bill, then he took a five-dollar bill from what was left and asked for her pen. As he wrote on it, she saw that the front of it was already covered with words. When he finished, he folded up the bill and reached out. She held up her hand to receive it. As he placed it there, he held her hand for a moment.

"Your answer is on this," he said. He started to pull away, but she held on. He stared through her. "I have nothing. The only thing I know for certain about my future is that I'll be at this little church on Sunday with my new friend Dale. I can't even remember the name of it."

"I'll find you," she said.

He slipped his hand out of hers, took a sip of cold coffee and grimaced. As he stood, he turned to look out the window. The rain had stopped, but clouds still covered the sky. He gripped the table as if taken with vertigo. Then he turned and walked away without looking back. She sat there watching out the window as he crossed the parking lot. He didn't stop at a car, didn't even look for one. He was telling the truth.

When she felt the pressure of time, she opened her hand and looked down at the five-dollar bill he had given her as a tip. In the top corner, it said, *Turn for a blessing.* She did so and saw all the phrases about God written there. When she had read them all, she turned it back over. Someone had written *Praise Jesus* on the front and Chris had drawn an arrow from that phrase to what he had written:

He told me

Lost, homeless, broken, Chris sat in this booth and watched her sit across from him and somehow, in some way, he believed Jesus had told him to talk to her? Did he know he was going to tell her his whole story? Had he ever told anyone else his story? Maybe it should have been weird, this crazy guy hearing the voice of Jesus. It wasn't. Strangely, she felt validated. A man who had no hope believed God had led him to tell Hope his story.

She looked down at Abraham Lincoln and decided two things. First, she would find Chris on Sunday morning. There were three churches in town, but she couldn't imagine Chris at St. Andrew's — the ritual would be too much all at once. Which narrowed it down to Beulah Community and Wesley Chapel. She would have to check the times of the services and decide what to do. Finding him again, letting him know someone cared about Chris, was the most important thing. Second, this five dollars would be the start of her college tuition account.

Hope had a funny feeling she was meant to reach people who needed her.

On a whim, she took out her pen and, underneath Chris's jagged letters, she wrote *My name is Hope.*

ZACH

Tap, tap, tap, tap.

I love Hope. Not in a weird way, you know? I don't, like, obsess about her. I just like her a lot. She's not like Theresa—not a bit. Theresa is cool, though. She's cool. She just likes the guys too much; you know? She couldn't ever just settle down with one guy and be okay. If I was her boyfriend, I'd be like, hey, Terry Berry, simmer down on the flirting, okay? Or I'll have to kill you.

Tap, tap, tap, tap.

I don't really mean that. It's just hard, you know? I have this job with all this responsibility and I have to keep everything going in there. How did I end up managing a restaurant? I thought I was going to be, like, a business man. An entrepreneur. But I'm not. I just babysit kids who are trying to make enough money to survive while they go on to better things. Servers and dishwashers and hosts who don't want restaurant work to be their whole lives. I don't want it to be my whole life, either; but it's not a bad life. I can afford what I need.

Tap, tap, tap, tap.

So anyway, I love Hope. Hey, in case you work in a restaurant, I'm not downing you. People got to eat, right? And you got to make money, right? Maybe being a restaurant manager is your whole life, and that's beautiful, man. It really is. If that's what you want to do with your life, go for it. Make the best of it. I personally think there's something amazing about helping a whole family have a great time together, put up their smartphones, talk to each other. Where else does that happen? When we eat at home, the TV is on, the games are playing, the earphones are on, all that. At a restaurant? Well, some people won't talk even then — but a lot of them do, you know? Very cool.

Tap, tap, tap, tap, tap.

What was I saying? Oh yeah. I love Hope. Here's some of the things I love about her. She doesn't need anybody. She doesn't, like, throw herself at every guy or even get to be friends with every girl. She's choosy. Like she has something to give every person in her life, so why bring so many people in that it wears you out? So she's picky. She likes you? You're gonna know it because she includes you. She doesn't like you? You're gonna know it because she doesn't. She's not rude. If she was rude, I'd probably back hand her. I'm not a mean guy, I just . . . Sometimes I feel that way.

Tap, tap, tap, tap.

He should be here by now. Probably is. Watching me, watching the car, watching the road. They call him Spider. I call him Spider. Fits him. He's waiting in a dark corner, spinning his web; I didn't see him for what he was until I was caught.

Tap, tap, tap, tap, tap, tap, tap.

Hope. I even like her name. That's one thing I like. I say it and I light up, you know? Hope. Hope. Hope. She's pretty, too. Don't think that isn't part of it, because it is. But if she was, you know, ugly, I think I would still light up when I said her name. Hope. Fits her like Spider fits him. That would be a great match, Spider versus Hope. Only I don't want Hope to meet Spider. Ever. She deserves better. I don't. I used to, but I don't now. Why isn't he here?

Tap, tap, tap, tap.

She was sitting with this guy today for a long time. Hope doesn't do that. She included him, so she must like him. She must see something in him. I took it as long as I could, then I had to get her to go back to work. The way she looked at him was hurting me. I wanted to close her eyes. What if she looked at me that way? I'd melt. I'd be a puddle at her feet, begging her to stop. I wouldn't mean it. I would want her to go on looking at me like that until I was free. But I'd be afraid she would know. I don't want anyone to know.

Tap, tap, tap, tap.

I'd probably kill myself. I'm kind of thinking about it now. Sometimes I think it would be easier. Hope wouldn't like that. I don't think she would. What would I care? Actually, I would care a lot. I'd be, like, a ghost, watching her think about me that way. Maybe she's the only reason I'm still alive. I don't really feel alive most of the time. Sometimes I do. If Spider gets here I will. If Hope looks at me that way I will.

Tap, tap, tap.

Headlights. If they pass by, I'm going to start my car and go home. It's, like, after two in the morning and I'm starting to feel it under my skin. If they pass by, I'm going to start the car and follow them. I won't do anything. I'll just follow them until they turn in their driveway and then I'll go home. I just want to go home. Don't. Stop it. Hope doesn't like people who feel sorry for themselves, either. I do. I feel sorry for me.

Tap, tap, tap.

If it wasn't so late, I'd start the car and play some music. Can't draw attention to myself, though. Cops come through here all the time, don't they? Often enough. Shoot. They passed me by. Not him. The Spider isn't coming, I guess, and those people are probably just on their way home from a bar. They had a good time tonight, I bet. I want to start the car and follow them home, but I have to stay here. Spider might show up yet. I need the Spider.

Tap, tap, tap, tap, tap.

I'm sorry; I know it's annoying. I just can't stop. Drumming on the steering wheel keeps me from doing other stupid stuff. I want to stop because now it's annoying me. Spider is annoying me. He knows he doesn't have to be here on time because he knows I'll wait as long as I have to. What else am I going to do? I need to find somebody else who can give me life. Who am I kidding? Anyone who has what Spider has would probably treat me the same way. Makes me want to hurt somebody.

Tap, tap, tap, tap, tap, tap, tap, tap, tap.

The cigarette helps, but not much. How long has it been? How stupid was it to try to do this on my own? Three days, four? I just wanted to get free. I wanted to have hope. Hope. Yeah, I want her to be mine, too, because she would understand. She would. I could go to her and tell her and she would get it. She wouldn't know what I was feeling, but she would feel me feeling it. And I want that. I want someone to feel me feeling it.

It's been four days now. I was off for the first two and thought maybe I had it licked. Then I went to work — stupid decision, but I had to — and right there, in the middle of the restaurant, I realized I couldn't do it. Yesterday. No, wait, now it's day before yesterday. Two days ago, I stood at the place where I'm the boss and everyone is relying on me and I needed it so bad I thought I would pass out or vomit or something.

Tap, tap, tap, tap.

Know who noticed, don't you? Not Terry Berry. Not that one. She just looked at me and rolled her eyes and went to drop off some food at one of her tables. No one else even saw it happening. Hope. Hope looked up from the cup of ice she had just started filling with iced tea and saw me. She asked if I was okay. I said I just felt dizzy for a moment, but that wasn't true. I felt unreal. Fake. Dead breathing. I said I felt dizzy, and she dropped everything and took my elbow and helped me back to the break room. When I sat down, I wanted to roll up my sleeve. Then I remembered where I was. Who was there. Hope.

Tap, tap, tap, tap.

I almost blew it. Ha! Stupid. I put my head down on my arms and leaned into the table. She put a hand on the back of my neck. Checking for fever? I don't know. But it felt good. It felt real. Like an anchor feels real. She stood there for a moment and then told me to take as long as I needed. When she left, the room smelled different. So I knew when she came back with a wet dish towel because I could smell the difference. I looked up and she looked down at me but it was too quick. I didn't get to see what she was seeing. She told me she just had another table sit, but that when she got them drinks she would check on everybody for me.

Tap, tap, tap, tap, tap.

Know what else I like about Hope? She's cool. She didn't make a big deal about it. The break room was empty, so I called Spider. He said he was out and couldn't help me until he got more. When is that? Friday night. When can I see him? Go to the church after work, he said. That's what I did. I've been here since I finished the paperwork.

Well, I didn't finish the paperwork. I probably got here too early. Hope's cool. The next morning, she asked if I was feeling better. Wrong question, you know? She should have asked if I felt present. But she doesn't know. How could she? I did feel better, though, because I knew I was meeting Spider later. I could deal. One more night. I went to the bathroom after that and threw up.

Tap, tap, tap, tap.

I haven't slept since Wednesday. Can't. In my dreams, I hurt myself. I hurt people. I think I know what it means. I'm just that person, you know? The one who lets everybody down. The one who means nothing. If I disappeared, the restaurant would be like, oh well, I guess we gotta hire somebody new. My mom and dad would be like, oh well, guess we'll have to love our other son and our daughter more. Theresa would be like, oh well, guess I'll have to meet Spider for myself. So when I dream, I think about how I might hurt people but I'll probably only end up hurting myself. No one would spend too much time feeling sorry about it.

Tap, tap, tap.

Not Hope. Hope would be like, I knew something was wrong. She would be like, yeah, I thought he was hurting inside. She would know. She likes me. She included me. It's nice to feel included. It's nice to feel. I want so bad to tell her because I think she would help me. I would quit and she would be real, be my anchor, and I'd latch onto her and pray that my ship doesn't sink. And she'd think that was cool because she likes to pray before she eats.

Hope is the kind of religious person I like. She doesn't tell me how I should think about God. She just goes on about her Godthinking on her own. Then you ask her and she's, like, I don't know. My Momma always told me to be thankful. I'm thankful. Her Momma has a lot do with Hope being here.

Tap, tap, tap, tap, tap, tap, tap.

More headlights coming. Oh no. Cop. He won't stop if I scrunch down and disappear. He won't stop. He won't stop. Did I hear him braking? Did he turn into the parking lot? Oh, man. Why am I here? What's my story?

My girlfriend Theresa just broke up with me. I'm just upset. Cry. Cry! If I blink my eyes real fast, they will water and it'll look like I've been crying. I'm not hiding, I'm laying down. I'm tired, but I don't want to go home. She lives with me, yeah, and she's getting her stuff. Maybe he will want to follow me home to make sure, but that's okay. Her stuff won't be there. Ha! Don't laugh, cry.

Too long. Oh, man, I'm stupid! He never stopped or pulled in. Good.

Tap, tap, tap, tap, tap.

Why didn't I pray right then? Because God doesn't hear the prayers of a junkie. He doesn't hear them because junkies only pray for the next fix. There he is. I recognize Spider's car. Of course. I should have been looking for his car, not for headlights. What time is it? 2:48. He said he would meet me at three in the morning in the church parking lot. I remember now.

Hope will forgive me. She left her purse in the break room and I had to take some of her money. It's okay. She's cool, you know? I'll try to put it back in when she doesn't know it. She will be like, hey, there's that money I lost! I had to take it all, though. Spider says the price has gone up. I think he's punishing me for trying to stop. I want to hit him for it, but then where would I get my stuff? He wouldn't sell it to me anymore if I hit him.

Tap, tap, tap, tap.

I'm really not violent. It's just that since the last time I did heroin, I've been feeling that way. Kill myself, that would be the best idea. Sure, some people would feel some pain. But I wouldn't hurt anybody that way. Except Hope.

I wouldn't have Hope if I did that.

Here he comes. Here comes life. I already almost feel real. He can have all of my money if I can just feel real.

RUNNER

"Hey, look. Runner's here."

"What?"

Spider looked up, his eyelids droopy, as he untied the rubber from around his wrist. He squinted and then laughed. "Aw, man. I thought you were the runner."

He rubbed his good hand over his bald head and tugged at an ear lobe. Eyes closing, he leaned back into the dirty couch and let the drug travel from the vein in his hand through his body. For a while, the two young men were silent. Runner thought he was going to sleep.

Spider's eyes shot open. "You running for me now?"

"I thought Robbie was running for you."

"Mmm…" Spider mused, then made himself sit forward. "Yeah, yeah. He did. He does. But he's temporarily indisposed."

"What you mean is Robbie finally let you shoot him up."

Spider laughed. "Yeah, that's it. See? You're smart enough to be a runner. Be my runner."

The two young men were silent again, but the air had changed. Suddenly, Spider was business and the other was nervous. A yes to become Runner usually meant two things: a cut of the profits and a path to using. Every Runner before expected to take advantage of the good part and say no to the bad part. Robbie was not the first Runner to fall.

"Runner, I've got a drop off that needs to be made in about half an hour. The dude is going to be waiting in the parking lot of the little country church out on Highway 256. Know the one I mean?" Runner was silent. "Yeah, you know. He'll give you all the money he's got. You give him the good stuff. Use my car, come back and you get twenty percent of what you bring."

A woman walked into the living room from the dark hallway. Runner looked up at her. She had stringy blonde hair, red splotches on her face, very thin. The shorts and T-shirt she wore were too big to be hers and she was barefoot. She never looked at either of them, just walked through the room, through the screen door, and out onto the lawn.

"Wendy, get back here!"

Runner looked over his shoulder through the door. "That was Wendy?"

"Yeah," Spider grunted. "I kinda feel bad about that."

"Wasn't she in rehab down near Beulah?" "Was."

Runner thought about saying no. He was already way past curfew, which was actually incentive to say yes. The later the better, at that point. Maybe he could call a friend and sneak in, tell his parents he forgot to call to tell them he was staying the night. He sure couldn't tell them about being at Spider's.

Spider. What a joke. Runner was a freshman when they met, Spider a junior. Back then he was Victor Bledsoe. Vic was a good guy, a cool guy. They became fast friends after playing intramural basketball together at the school. Three months later, Vic had bought him his first pack of cigarettes. Not long after, Vic had invited him to his first party and given him his first beer. Runner didn't just like him. He wanted to be Victor Bledsoe. When he started calling himself Spider, Runner started calling himself Snake. Snake wore off after a while, but Spider stuck.

Then Spider had become a runner. Then he used. Then he started dealing. Now, he was asking his friend to follow in his footsteps.

"How smart can I be?" Runner didn't wait for Spider to answer. He picked up the keys and the package and went out to the car. Opening the trunk, he pulled up the liner hiding the spare and put the package under both. Walking around the car and sliding behind the wheel, Runner slid the key in the ignition and brought the engine to life.

Lights on. Check the mirrors. Oh, seatbelt. Adjust the seat, check the mirrors again. Drive.

Zach popped out of his car as soon as the driver came to a stop and turned off the headlights. He knew he needed to keep a low profile, but he was anxious to get the stuff and get home. Can't shoot up in the parking lot. Can't take a chance driving that way.

The driver didn't move. He was clutching the steering wheel with both hands. Bending down to get a better look, Zach saw that it was a kid—a teenager, probably hadn't had his license very long. Where was Robbie? Where was Spider?

He thought about going around to the driver side like he usually did, but Zach wondered if this was a set up. What if this kid was a part of a sting? Looking right and left, he peered into the darkness. Nothing and no one in sight. If the police were involved, they sure left this boy off to himself. Shaking his head, Zach rubbed his hands together and bent down again.

"You the one meeting me?" he asked. No movement from inside the car. "You the new runner?"

Was he scaring the kid? To set him at ease, Zach turned around and reached through his window to pull out Hope's tips for the day. He heard the car kick into gear and pull back from him. Holding the money up in one hand and his other hand in plain view, Zach frantically waved at the boy.

"No, no, don't leave! I'm just getting my money, okay?" Headlights blazed, stinging Zach's eyes. He blinked rapidly as they adjusted for the intense glare. Trying to keep his elbows out and his hands in front of him, Zach looked down at the bills in his hand. She had written on the top one, "My name is Hope."

The lights went off and now Zach was blind. She had written her name on it. Why? Had she suspected what he would do? Had she known she was the only reason he was clinging to life? Was she sending him a message?

My name is Hope.

The car door opened. He barely made out the kid standing there, foppish blonde hair spilling over his eyes. This runner was skittish. Probably a rookie. Zach took a deep breath as he imagined the rush of reality to be his soon . . .

My name is Hope.

. . . the rush of reality that would forever seal him off from her. Zach hung his head as he admitted he was never going to pay her back; that he would steal from her again. When she found out, he knew what would happen. When his boss found out, he knew what would happen. When the police found out, he knew what would happen.

"If I do this again, I know what will happen."

"You Zach?"

Zach looked up, nodded.

The runner walking toward the back of the car. "I've got what you need."

"Do you use?"

The runner stopped, turned. Shook his head, then hung it.

"Don't do it."

"I'm not." "Yet."

Silence answered.

"I know this person named Hope," Zach said. "I want to quit for Hope."

The boy looked up. "Then why are you here?" "To use the money I stole from Hope to buy my fix."

Turning toward the back of the car again, the runner took another step. "Like I said, I've got it."

"Will you help me?"

"Dude, I've got the stuff."

"No. Will you help me?"

Runner pulled out of the parking lot, watching the man out of the corner of his eye. The dude kicked at the panel under the glove compartment in a steady rhythm, rubbing his fingers over a five-dollar bill. The rest of the money was in Runner's pocket.

What was he doing? Spider was going to kill him! Well, maybe not kill him. Brushing blonde hair back out of his eyes, Runner slowed down to take the curve and then sped up again. Zach had started tapping on the console between them. Stealing a glance, he saw the sheen of perspiration on the man's forehead as they passed under a streetlight.

Spider wouldn't kill him. He had the money, and he could even return the dope. He could still say no to running. After all, he hadn't actually dealt to anyone. Yet.

"I'm gonna talk, okay?"

"What?"

The man rubbed his face. "I need to talk because talking will help me remember why I'm doing this."

"Well, start with where I turn next."

Zach laughed. "Yeah, good idea. Just past Beulah, before you get to the outskirts of the next town, there's a Joe Tiller Road."

"I think I know where that is."

Rubbing the five again, Zach said, "The rehab place is about ten miles north up that road as you get closer to the city."

Runner put his elbow on the door to his left. Their windows were down because the air conditioning had made Zach too cold. What time was it? The clock on the dash said 3:16. Spider would be expecting him in the next fifteen minutes. How far was he from the house? He wasn't experienced enough to estimate well, but he thought once he dropped Zach off he would be thirty minutes away. If things went smoothly with the rehab place, Runner still wouldn't get back before four.

"I keep looking at you and wondering how you got mixed up with heroin so young."

"I'm not . . ." Runner started to say, but Zach wasn't expecting an answer.

"I mean, what kind of idiot asks you to risk your life to run drugs for him? Do you use?"

"No. I told you that already."

Zach smiled and nodded. "Good. My name is Hope my name is Hope my name is Hope." The whispered mantra continued as they buzzed along the highway running through Beulah. Runner checked his speed as they got close to town. The last thing he needed was a cop pulling him over for speeding. Somewhere in the next mile, the speed limit dropped from 55 to 35 miles per hour. To be safe, Runner slowed a little more.

"Do you think one person can change your life? I do. I think everybody in the world is, like, waiting for that one person. I mean, one person changed my life when he convinced me to shoot up the first time.

"I was doing okay, you know? Managing at the restaurant is, like, good money, right? And I was about to ask this girl to marry me. Hours were horrendous, though. We didn't get to start having a social life until after midnight.

"At first we spent time together or with some friends from school. Then we got invited to some parties and started going out every weekend. That's when this guy told me he had something better and faster than alcohol. I thought it would be, like, I don't know, marijuana or something. Or maybe some prescription pills. We went into the bathroom and he started tying this rubber tube around his arm."

Zach wiped the sweat from his forehead on the cuff of his dress shirt. The moisture somehow brought out the smell of old, stale food. Runner swallowed the lump in his throat as he drove through the light at Fremont in front of the Wal-Mart. They were passing through the business district now. He had to drive carefully.

"Can you turn on the air? I'm hot." Knowing a reminder that the a/c had been on five minutes ago wouldn't do any good, Runner reached for the button. Zach rolled up his window and fiddled with the vent so it blew on his face. Then he continued, "I almost passed out watching him. Told him I didn't want to do it and didn't want to know he was doing it. I left the bathroom and went looking for my girl.

"Two weeks later we were at the same house and I had to pee. I went to the bathroom and you know who was in there? That guy and my girl. She was smiling at me when she said, 'He says it's an amazing high.' He was right. I mean, I had to join them, right?

"That was six months ago. Her name is Wendy. She's with him now."

Runner started to breathe easier as Beulah came to an end. The police would be lurking still, but at least they weren't driving straight through town extending an invitation. How far past the end of Beulah was Joe Tiller Road? Five miles? If the rehab place was almost to the city, it had to be another twenty minutes. As they passed a side road, a car rolled to a stop at the intersection and then turned behind them.

"I guess I went off the deep end for a while," Zach said. "I've been doing heroin since then, but this is the third time I've tried to stop."

"How long did you last the first time?"

Zach laughed. "Four days, eight hours, about twenty minutes. My stomach was so messed up. I stayed in the bathroom a lot, man. Got these incredible cramps in my calves. The shakes, the hot and cold, the works. I couldn't take it anymore. The second time was a forced stop. Spider ran out of junk and I couldn't find another buyer. That was about four days, too."

"He makes it up," Runner said, then bit his lip.

"What?"

Knowing he shouldn't continue, Runner found himself talking anyway. "He tells you he doesn't have the stuff because he knows you'll pay more for it if you need it. Not everybody. Just the ones with more money to spend. He can tell when you start running out of money."

"How?" Runner looked at Zach. "You start stealing from your waitresses."

"Servers."

"Whatever."

Tapping on the arm rest more, Zach looked out the window. A shudder coursed through him before he kicked again. He crossed his arms over his chest, then reached out to make the vent blow away from his face. Runner slowed as he caught sight of the sign for Joe Tiller Road. The car behind them was now only about seventy feet back.

"You said north, right? That's left?"

"Right, man. I mean, correct. Turn left."

Runner had just clicked on his right turn signal. Caught off guard, he braked a little harder than he needed and slammed the lever all the way down to signal left. He overcorrected a little bit but managed to turn onto the new road. Ten more miles, and he would be free of this guy. Looking in his rear view mirror, he saw the headlights of the car behind him.

"So it's in the trunk."

Runner gripped the steering wheel tightly. He had worried this might happen, but what could he have done? After seeing Wendy, he knew what was in store for this guy if he didn't get help. Despite the risk—from Spider and a random police stop, but also from Zach changing his mind—he felt compelled to help.

"The stuff I mean. The heroin. It's in the trunk."

"Yeah," Runner admitted. Then, because he had a feeling Spider wouldn't like it, he added, "This time. We change it up so you can't just get it."

Drumming on the glove compartment, Zach whispered, "My name is Hope my name is Hope my name is Hope."

"Tell me about Hope," Runner said.

"I don't want to talk about it right now. Hey, how am I going to get my car? I mean, if I go into this rehab place what will happen to it?"

"I hadn't thought of it."

"Dude, I can't let it get towed. Maybe you better take me back."

Runner looked over at him as they passed under a street light, saw how glassy the man's eyes were. "We'll be there in ten minutes. I'll take care of your car after you check in."

"It's not really a good idea. Hey, can we go back and get my car? Here, you can have this five dollars for gas."

Thrusting the five under Runner's hand, Zach retreated so his back was against the passenger side door. He was starting to shake. Crumpling the five so he wouldn't drop it, Runner extended it toward Zach.

"You already paid for my gas, Zach."

"No, it's yours. I already paid you. You know what? I already paid you. How about you just give me the stuff and take me back to my car."

"Zach, we're almost there."

"I don't want to go."

"Hope wants you to go."

He snorted. "Hope doesn't care about me. I'm an addict and a thief."

Red and blue lights began flashing behind them. Runner cursed under his breath and looked up at the rear view mirror.

The turn.

If he had made a smooth turn, the cop would have driven on down 256 and left them alone. He couldn't think. Should he pull over? After all, he was helping a guy go to rehab. How did they know each other? *Oh, officer, it's all good. I was going to sell this dope to this guy, but then we thought, why don't we just drive to rehab in the middle of the night.* Were they even open?

Suddenly, Zach reached out and grabbed the steering wheel. When he did, he forced the car to dive to the left. Runner tried to wrest control from him as they dipped down into a ditch. Dirt kicked up in the air as the front left of the bumper dug into the ground. They were going fast enough for the car to power through the embankment and the fence, but not the tree.

Turned sideways, Zach wasn't held in check by his seat belt. He slammed into the dash and back into the seat, then careened into the passenger side window. Somehow, he completely missed the runner. The airbag did not.

Chest hurting, head exploding, looking down, the last thing Little Chet saw was the five-dollar bill clutched in his hand.

YOU

By the time you pull into the parking lot, your foot is throbbing. The clinic was only a fifteen-minute drive so you thought pressing on the pedals with a broken foot wouldn't matter. Well, possibly broken foot—you don't know for certain. Hence the trip. But the clinic was full of people with the stomach flu and nurses with a mound of paperwork. You decided you couldn't wait, so you left the clinic and drove to the emergency room.

An hour after dropping the entertainment center on your foot, you hobble into the emergency room. Every step creates fire up your calf, but you're committed now. The door slides open and a blast of cool air washes over you. Why do all hospitals smell the same? You look around the waiting room and can't believe your eyes. Stomach flu, others coughing and wheezing, a bleeding cut. You should have stayed at the clinic!

At the counter, you have to explain your foot hurts (no one could tell by the limp). The lady is nice enough as she takes your information, but she tells you she will call you when a spot opens up with their — what did she call it — their information gatherer people. She directs you to please sit down. Looking at her name tag, you thank Alyssa and hobble over to an empty chair that isn't near someone who might throw up. That's when a real emergency shows up. A gurney comes in off an ambulance, followed by a second.

An hour later, you go up to Alyssa and tell her your foot is going to fall off. She holds up a finger for you to wait, finishes her phone call, then apologizes. She asks you to take your seat and she will be with you in a moment. Despite the heat rising into your cheeks, you go back to your seat and decide you're giving them ten minutes.

Fifteen minutes later a nurse kneels down in front of you. She has an ice pack and two ibuprofen, explains that they've had two car accidents in the last four hours and a round of flu. Apologizing again, she offers a wheel chair to help you over to patient services. By this time your foot is numb and swollen, but you know if you try to walk on it the pain will return. This nurse, Anna, gives you support as you shift into the wheel chair. She pushes you to a cubicle where you give everything but a sample of your blood to an elderly lady named Adeline.

Just as you think only females with names that start with "A" can work there, a young man named Ray collects you and takes you back toward the examination rooms. That's when Ray finds out the person in ER-12 hasn't left yet. He sets you next to the wall between your future room and ER-11 and tells you he's going to check on it and will be right back.

Twenty minutes later, you're about to get up and walk out. The ice pack is warm, the ibuprofen is wearing thin and so is your temper. That's when a police officer walks down a hall and stops at ER-11. He nods to you, then walks inside. Though he pulls the door closed behind him, he doesn't realize he's left it open a crack. Someone inside asks him a question, but it's a low buzz. Your officer is a tenor. When he answers, you can hear every word.

"I don't know, John. I think the boy is telling the truth."

Buzz. Buzz. Burr.

Your officer laughs. "Oh, no, I mean about not doing drugs. We took some blood, so we'll know soon enough. We found the other perp's car at a church up the highway. They probably met there."

Burr. Burr. Buzz.

"Yes, but I bet he was set up. He has no criminal record and I think the toxicology is going to come back clean."

You can't help yourself. You lean in a little and listen harder. The other man in the room says, "What do you want to do?"

"Scare him a little. He took some money, but they were on the road, heading toward the rehab clinic. Eighty percent of his story checks out. If we give him something to think about, my guess is he'll avoid the other twenty percent from now on."

"Did he tell you where he got it?" "He didn't have to. Car belongs to Victor Bledsoe."

"Spider let him drive the car?"

Your officer laughs again. "Yeah, and the kid trashed it and gave us a string we can follow to him. You ready to do this?"

The door is starting to open, so you lean further over in your chair and adjust your warm ice pack. The first cop doesn't even look at you as he walks around you to ER-12. The second one gives you a glance as you settle back. He nods at you and asks you to excuse them. When they are both in the room, they close the door all the way.

Annoyed but also feeling a bit guilty, you look around for Ray. That's when you see a man in golf clothes and a woman in jeans and a t-shirt hustling your way. They stop Ray — there he is — and ask where they can find their son, Chester. They are led to — you guessed it — the room right next to you. When they open the door, your officer meets them.

"Mr. and Mrs. Spaulding?"

"Is my son in there?"

The officer steps out of the way so Mister Spaulding can go inside. Mrs. Spaulding follows. As you hoped, no one closes the door. You sit back against the wall so you can hear better. That's when Ray walks over with a doctor in tow. They take you into ER-11 and close the door.

For the third time, you explain you were moving the entertainment center without a dolly, lost your grip, and the full weight came right down on your foot. They take off the shoe and sock to see it is already swollen and purple. X-rays are in your near future. You are given stronger pain medicine and a new ice pack.

When they are gone, your mind wanders back to Chester Spaulding. What happened to him? If his mom and dad came to see him, he couldn't be more than fifteen or sixteen.

No, seventeen or eighteen; old enough to drive. He crashed the car of a guy whose nickname is Spider. That can't be good. As you think about the exchange, you remember they recognized Spider's real name and weren't surprised to hear him attached to the drug scene.

Heroin. You aren't sure, but you remember hearing that a community west of Beulah has seen a rise in heroin addiction. How did they get all the way over here? The rehab place. Must be talking about Living Hope over on Joe Tiller Road. What happened? Was he taking someone there? Why? The cop said they found the other man's car in a church parking lot. Had they met there for a drug deal?

You can't imagine it. Getting into drug deals at seventeen years old? The drugs and the ice are starting to take effect when Ray comes to cart you down to radiology. Twenty painful minutes later, you are back in your exam room waiting. The police are gone, but the Spauldings are still in ER-12. The doctor comes in and tells you the foot is not broken but very bruised. They give you the option to wrap it with a bandage or get a boot for it. You always wanted a boot for when you do other stupid stuff to your body, so you go for the boot.

After nodding in all the right places about how to use it, you let them put it on you. Some paperwork needs your signature and then Anna comes to wheel you back out to the waiting room. Mr. and Mrs. Spaulding are out there, talking to your officer at the door.

You look over and see a blonde-haired young man, about the right age. He's looking down at something in his hands. Someone calls for Anna before you reach the door. She asks for your patience and leaves you in front of Chester as she steps over to the counter to answer a question.

You are close enough that you can see he has a five-dollar bill in his hand. It's been through a lot, wrinkled with a corner torn off. You notice handwriting on it and you are trying to read it when Chester looks up at you.

Your eyes meet. His are watery, bloodshot. He looks tired. The teenage version of a five o'clock shadow is growing around his chin and he has a bruise on his forehead. You can't break the eye contact. For a moment, you consider saying something; but what? That you eavesdropped on a conversation the police were having about him? That you know he's into something bad and needs to stay out? Maybe, you think, it's better not to get involved. You're suddenly praying Anna comes back soon when he pushes his fingers through the mop of hair and returns your gaze.

"He said he wanted to quit for someone named Hope," Chester says. You don't know if he even sees you, don't know if you should respond. He looks down at the five-dollar bill, smooths it out, and holds it up for you to see that several people have written on the front. He points to the relevant phrases and your breath catches.

Praise Jesus, with an arrow down to another phrase written by someone else, *He told me*, and below that, in a third hand, *My name is Hope.*

Praise Jesus, He told me My name is Hope.

Before you can say anything, Anna comes back and wheels you outside. She's nice enough to take you all the way to your car and help you into the driver's seat. You make a joke about never driving in boots and she laughs. She tells you to be very careful going home and reminds you of the doctor's instructions. When she's gone, you turn the key in the ignition and the engine roars to life. The radio comes on, playing a little loudly. You turn it off. And sit.

The story comes into focus a little bit. A teenage boy caught in a drug scene but not yet taking them. He's asked to meet someone and make a deal, but when he gets there the guy wants help getting to Living Hope rehab. Somehow they get into an accident, but not before the addict tells the boy he wants to quit for some girl named Hope.

But that's not what the boy hears. He hears Jesus calling him.

"God," you whisper, "if you're listening, help that boy."

Your foot aches when you step on the gas, but you've got to get a prescription filled before you can go home and rest. Unable to stop yourself, you wonder what else was written on that money.

JAMES

Gravel spat out from under the tires as he spun the wheel and looked over his shoulder to back into his usual spot. For the last twelve years, he had parked in the rear to allow space for visitors. For the last six years, his best friends joked with him about it. Vaughn Pinckney was a good man, but he had a nasty sense of humor.

"Making room for ghosts or invisible super heroes?"

"Making room for visitors, Vaughn."

"Ghosts, then."

As the late model Buick settled into its normal place, James turned off the engine. He pulled the keys into his lap and stared at them. For the first time, he let himself consider Vaughn was right. The hands fiddling with the key ring were gnarled, busted knuckles paying homage to thirty years as a mechanic. He retired four years ago but still couldn't get all the grease off them.

James let his eyes wander over the clothes he had chosen this morning. He felt uncomfortable in the casual slacks and button-up shirt. For the first time, he was showing up in church without wearing a suit. No doubt Pastor Preston's eyes would light up.

"Shows how desperate I am, I guess," James said. He looked at the clock on the dash board. 7:15 am, two hours before Sunday School started. Sighing, he wondered what he was doing here. Vaughn and his wife set up the communion trays last night. Jason printed the bulletins earlier in the week and Pastor Preston's wife had cleaned the church. All he needed to do was turn the lights on and make sure the a/c was working.

Looking up, he caught a glimpse of Pastor Preston's beat up old car parked at the side. Next to it was Jason's car. He chuckled. Whatever fate was in store for Beulah Community Church, those two boys would go down swinging. What could they be doing this early that they couldn't have done earlier in the week?

Taking a deep breath, James looked in the rear view mirror and straightened his collar. "No way to think of your spiritual leader," he told himself. Spiritual leader. The boy wasn't old enough to understand what that meant yet. Jason was younger still. A sudden wave of guilt swept over him as he stared into the deep green eyes that moistened as he watched them. Why had they let those boys come here? Soon they wouldn't be able to pay the salary of the first, wouldn't be able to hold on to the second. Beulah didn't deserve either of them and they didn't deserve Beulah.

"When will you close our doors, Father?"

There. Said aloud, the culmination of his thoughts hung in the air. James couldn't face himself, so he turned his gaze toward the church building. Red brick with white mortar, dark shingles sloping to once-white gutters, it squatted where it had always been.

Seeing it with fresh eyes, James grimaced. No one had cut the grass this week. The bushes needed trimming. The wood on the wheel chair ramp was weathered and faded. The gutters needed cleaning—better, replacing. Was that a hole at the base near the cornerstone? How long had that been there?

Longer than he wanted to admit.

James realized the Lord was speaking to him. Four pastors in the last fifteen years, all good speakers, all with a heart for the lost. All gone. A hole in the foundation of the building and everyone wanted to blame a leaky roof for the mildew inside. He went through the list. Pastor Charles grew the church to a hundred before resigning because of an altercation with an elder. Pastor Ben reached out to the factory workers on the edge of town before leaving because of a rumored affair—one he vehemently denied. Pastor Wayne brought them their most recent heyday, filling the church with nearly two hundred for Easter. He left when the leadership voted against going to two services. Pastor Henry . . .

"I'm sorry, Lord," James said. "Even now I don't think we always did the wrong thing. I just wish I had taken the time to get the other side of those stories."

A hole in the foundation, and every time they believed the issue was the pastor. Yet the common denominator was not the man in the pulpit. James shook his head, trying to clear his thoughts. This was Facebook's fault. If he had never learned to use social media, he would have missed Mary Parkinson's post last night. He ran a hand through the salt and pepper hair and let it rest on the nape of his neck. Adjusting in his seat, he took his smartphone out of his pocket. A couple of taps and the page was up.

Mary Parkinson *I had a chance to be the church this week and blew it. I don't even know what happened. All I know is that for the last 3 days I can't think of anything else. What are we doing on Sunday? I wish I could say we are . . .* **See More**

James let his thumb hover over the "See More" of the post. He almost knew the rest by heart anyway. Last night it was embedded between pictures of his grandkids and a meme that said *Type Amen if you love Jesus, scroll past if you don't!* He had almost skipped it. In a way, he wished he had; in a way, he was glad he didn't. Pressing down, he scanned the rest of the long confession and scrolled to the end where she had written,

> *I can't help thinking about what church is. I mean, people who gather to worship God in countries where they could be killed for doing it aren't getting together to study the Bible. Well, they are, but for a purpose. They are coming together to talk about how they can reach one more, teach one more, help one more grow in Christ. Maybe that's why we're struggling. It doesn't cost us anything anymore. I want to be part of something. I want to make a difference. God, help me make a difference starting now.*

This time, the tear escaped. Her cry was an echo to his, but he suddenly didn't want to "See More." The epiphany was too painful.

She had brought it to completion, but he had to be honest with himself. The extra five Dolores put in the plate the previous week made James question his commitment to the mission of Christ.

James loved his church. He loved Preston the way he had loved Charles, Ben, Wayne, and Henry. More so, because he was so young and enthusiastic. He loved coming early, serving communion, taking and counting the offering. He loved seeing his friends, having coffee with them. He loved mixing it up in the class room over passages in the Bible, loved hearing good preaching. This had become church to him. Was it something more?

The front door opened and the two young men stepped out together, heads bowed as they walked. Preston's mouth was moving, his face screwed into a painful, mournful fit of passion as he spoke. When he stopped, Jason's mouth began working. For a moment, their hands brushed and he saw Jason grab his friend's hand and stop him. They stood before the church, Jason facing his pastor, placing a hand on Preston's shoulder.

They were praying.

Did they do this every Sunday? His cheeks were wet. He set the phone in his lap and used both hands to scrub his face. Reaching into the glove compartment, he rifled through paperwork and pulled out tissues. Wiping his eyes and blowing his nose, he looked back at himself in the rear view mirror.

"Today, God," he said as he glared at the reflection.

Tossing the tissue on the floor board, James grabbed his Bible out of the passenger seat. He stepped out of the car and slammed his door shut. At the sound, the two young men looked over and waved at him. He lifted his Bible in salute. Instead of waiting for him, they turned and began walking around the church building. Praying.

James went up the front walk but took the walkway to the right of the church toward the storage shed. Turning the combination and yanking open the lock, he stepped inside and grabbed the key to the lawn tractor. Setting the Bible on a shelf, he saddled up and started the engine. In a puff of smoke, he was out the door and running down the grass. For some reason, he wanted the lawn to look better than it ever had this morning.

The rhythm of the job got to him. His mind wandered over the commitments in his life, the responsibilities weighing on him. He lost himself in the noise of the tractor, the organized disappearance of the disheveled yard. Row by row, slowly, carefully, he brought order to the chaos. Finally, his mind was quiet. Not numb, quiet. He smiled as he urged the machine down the last row and ended near the shed. Turning around and backing up, he returned the tractor to its place. Grabbing the leaf blower, he stepped out of the shed and saw his niece's little sports car pull up. Seth got out on the passenger side and walked around the car. He talked to his sister for a minute, then turned to wave at Uncle James. Returning the wave, James pulled the cord and started up the contraption in his hands. He saw Blaise emerge from her side of the car as he turned to sweep the grass off the walk and the front of the parking lot.

Father, he prayed as he watched the rush of air do its job, *may your Holy Spirit blow through us, move us from where we are to where we need to be. Start with my little niece, if You will.*

He finished by 8:15, not much worse for wear except for sweat from hauling the blower around. A golf shirt lay in the back seat of his Buick, so he went out and retrieved it. Now Vaughn would really have something to talk about. The front door of the church was open, as always, and James' mind returned to Pastor Preston and his protégé. Were they always praying so early at the church, or was this a special Sunday?

He walked through the small foyer intending to pass through the sanctuary to Preston's little office behind the stage. *Why did we hide our pastor back there?* He was so caught by the thought that he almost missed the two teenagers kneeling at the steps before the pulpit. Seth had his arm around his sister and she was sobbing and saying "I'm sorry, Seth, I'm so sorry."

Go to them.

He didn't hesitate. Crossing between pews, he made it to the center aisle and walked the same path he had walked to accept Christ as his savior. Grunting, he knelt down on the other side of Blaise and put his hand on her shoulder. She seemed to relax under the touch. James looked past her to Seth and saw the grateful look in his eyes. Bowing his head, James let his heart settle in his chest.

"Father, this is my niece and I love her. She means the world to me and nothing she has or could ever do will change that. She is family, and she is special. She may not know it, but I pray for her all the time. I love her. I would die for her if I could take this pain away.

"But my love for her is nothing compared to Your love for her. She is Your daughter. She means the world to You and nothing she has or could ever do will change that. She is family, and she is special. She may not know it, but Jesus intercedes for her all the time. He loves her, and He did die for her to take this pain away.

"Whatever is burdening her heart, I pray you release her fear and help her see Your love and grace. You bless those who do right, but You also forgive those who do wrong."

At those words, he felt Blaise jerk under his hand. He sensed rather than saw her head turn toward him, so he paused and opened his eyes to look at her. The wonder on her face made him laugh out loud. At his chuckle, she smiled.

"Did you read that somewhere, Uncle James?"

Arching an eyebrow, James replied, "Yes, Blaise. In the Bible."

Wiping her eyes, Blaise threw her arms around him and squeezed him so tightly that his breath left him. Seth hugged her from behind as the three of them melted into one. James thought of the Trinity--the Spirit that led him to this moment, the grace bestowed on them by the Father, the blessedness of serving Jesus. When Blaise pulled away, she dug into the back pocket of her jeans and handed a wad of money to Seth. He looked at her and nodded, taking it.

"Go get your game, little brother."

"I will. And some day I'm going to teach a little person how to play on it."

Blaise barked a laugh and then covered her mouth with her hand. "Count on it."

"I hate to break up this little private conference," James said, "but could someone help an old man up off his knees?"

Joy filled the room as the giggling teenagers each took an arm and helped him stand up. Blaise hugged him again and whispered a thank you in his ear, then turned and punched her brother in the shoulder. They walked out, talking in low voices. Appearing at the door to his office, Preston looked after them, loving them. His mouth moved without sound. James watched his pastor do the work of a spiritual leader and felt fresh guilt for his earlier thoughts. Perhaps this young man was old enough to know what it meant, after all. As James walked toward his pastor, he realized they hadn't said amen after the prayer.

Maybe that was all right. Maybe the prayer wasn't finished.

"A golf shirt, Mr. Randolph?"

"I knew you'd be pleased," James said, smiling.

JASON

PRAYER JOURNAL: Jason Nickerson

March 29, 2015

Preston preached about prayer today. He said a prayer journal is a good way to keep track of what God is doing in our lives. What prayers He has answered, what prayers we are glad He didn't answer. I've never been much for journaling, but I promised Preston I would try. He's been here since January and is actually a pretty good speaker. I would never have guessed it when we were in college together.

Requests:

1. A desire to draw closer to Jesus.
2. A way to serve Jesus with my gifts.
3. A life fulfilling in Christ.
4. Someone to share it with.
5. A new start financially.

Amen.

April 5, 2015

Decided to do this journal thing every Sunday after church. It's easier than trying to do it every day. I looked at what I wrote last week and it's too clinical and too selfish. I wish I knew how to make it more personal. What can I say? I like lists. I'm an artist with a guitar in my hand but put a pen in my hand and I become an engineer.

Requests:

1. A desire to seek out the needs of others and pray for them.
2. All the stuff I wrote last week.

Amen.

April 19th, 2015

Okay, I'm terrible at this. It's like after church I have had enough of the Christian stuff and last week I just didn't want to write anything. I don't know if this is working. I'm trying to "fake it till I make it."

Requests:

1. Pastor Preston to find a full time job. (Weird to think of him as my pastor!)
2. All that other stuff I'm praying for.

I don't think it helps anything to keep writing down the same stuff over and over.

Wait, who am I explaining this to? God? Dear reader? Myself? What was it Pastor said about prayer? Become aware of God, acknowledge His presence and power in my life, align myself with His will. Is that what I'm doing in this journal?

    3. Learn to pray.

Amen.

April 26, 2015

Preston asked me to be the regular worship leader today. I've been playing guitar and leading the singing at Beulah Community since Eunice Staley died. She was a nice lady, played the organ and piano there for over thirty years. Couldn't carry a tune in a bucket, but everybody loved her. I went to her funeral and couldn't believe the number of people who came to pay their respects. Who knew an organ player could have such an impact on the lives of so many people?

Of course it was more than the playing, but so many people made mention of their favorite song. Dolores Joyce said she and Chet loved "When I Survey the Wondrous Cross." I checked out the lyrics on Google and found out that's where Chris Tomlin got the lines for "The Wonderful Cross." He used the verses and added a chorus to it! Amazing.

Anyway, I've been filling in each week, learning some of the older hymns.

I never stepped foot in a church until I was almost twenty, so I don't know many of them. To be honest, I thought I was butchering them. Preston must think otherwise. I have to pray about what to do.

Wait. I've already been praying about it. It's been #2 on my list for a month!
God, thank you for answering my prayer. Can you see to the others now?

Amen.

June 14th, 2015
Wow. It's been almost two months since I used this journal. I didn't realize when I said yes to being the worship leader at Beulah that I was signing up to partner with Preston in such a big way. He believes the whole morning is worship, so he wants what I do and what he does to mesh. That means my Sundays are suddenly very busy. I'm meeting him on Wednesday nights now, too, to talk about where his sermon is taking him so I know what songs to pick. Since I'm usually not working at the plant on Thursdays, I'm doing the bulletins now on that day, too.

Requests:

1. Pastor Preston finds a better job. (I guess his part time gig is an answer to prayer, but he and his wife are still struggling.)
2. The leadership of Beulah starts seeing the vision God has given the Pastor.
3. God, I really, really, want to meet someone willing to share this journey with me.
4. Help us create an environment of worship at Beulah.
5. All the stuff from the first list (except how to use my gifts, thank you, God!).

Amen.

June 21st, 2015

I don't know if this is going to work. God, You are bigger than we are. You know what will bring this church to life. We don't have a clue. Well, I think Preston does.

He's getting frustrated, though. I think it's starting to leak into his faith a little. God, please help him to hear from You. He needs Your encouragement right now. Nothing is changing at the church, and he's preaching his heart out every Sunday. He asked me to start playing some faster tunes right before the offering. I think the money situation is getting to all the leaders, but the Pastor is the only one directly affected by the low giving.

Hey, I just prayed in my prayer journal!

Requests:

1. Bring this church to life.
2. Use Preston to do it.
3. Use me to do it.
4. Help us to do as Preston preached today: spur on the saints to good deeds!

I wonder what Preston would think if I asked him to start meeting me early on Sunday to pray for the church. He'd probably eat up the idea.

Amen.

August 23, 2015
God, my Father, the One who sees me and knows my heart, what are You doing? I met a girl today who has my stomach doing flip flops. She was stalled out in front of a Wal-Mart and I could see her starting to panic. When I jumped out to help her, I almost couldn't talk. Had some teens with me from the church and we were headed to watch a baseball game, but I walked her over to the auto parts store and helped her replace a battery.

Something happened there, too. Met a guy named Dave Graybill who manages the place. He said something about not going to church and quick as a wink I said, "What is church?" The question stunned him. Don't know where it came from, but I'm going to start using it more often. He was greatly affected by it. I think he gave Lianne a deal on that battery.

Lianne. Can't get her out of my head now. Even more so because of this weird experience with a five-dollar bill where she wrote on it that she believes in Jesus. I asked her to church, but now I feel guilty. I don't want to use the church or my position in it to impress chicks. Still, if she shows up next Sunday I won't know how to act.

Is this a prayer journal or a dear diary? Need to stop and focus on praying.

Requests:
1. Pastor Preston finds a job already. Please?
2. Thank you, God, for the desire to draw closer to you.

Wait. That's a second answer to prayer. God, I have felt a stronger urge to know You and serve You. Praise You, Jesus!

3. Bring David and his family to church, if he can work it out in his schedule.
4. And Lianne. Help me to focus on You on Sunday even if she shows up.
5. I want to be able to tithe, God. Help me do better with my money so I can help Preston.
6. Help me reach some of these teenagers. I see some growth in Seth.

Preston was SO right about this. Just realized another answer to prayer: I'm praying for other people!

Almost forgot. Preston and I have started praying together early Sunday mornings. Listen to our hearts, God. We want to reach Beulah for Jesus.

Amen.

August 25, 2015
Got a call from Seth tonight. He had a traumatic experience with an older gentleman today, then topped it off with a heart wrenching experience with his sister Blaise. She's pregnant and I think she's contemplating abortion. I called Preston to see what we should do and we prayed together over the phone.

God, I have to admit I feel like that's not enough. Isn't there more for us to do? Shouldn't I call her parents? Talk to her? Lay myself in front of the abortion clinic and grab at her ankles if she shows up and tries to walk in? Is prayer powerful enough to save that baby's life?

I pray it is, despite the irony of that statement. We really don't know for sure what's going on. If we talk to her parents, would she listen to them? If she isn't considering abortion, will talk about it make her think about it? All we can do is pray, so God we trust in Your Word and believe prayer is our greatest weapon.

Amen.

August 26, 2015
I cannot believe how COOL YOU ARE!

Okay, God, this is more for me to remember than any real prayer.

When I met with Preston tonight, he told me about this weird experience where God gave him a coupon and a five-dollar bill to get his hair cut just when he was questioning his own faith. (Answer to prayer #4! I was asking You to strengthen his faith, and You did!) That's awesome in itself, but then he starts talking about what was on the money and I freaked out. It was the same $5 that Lianne wrote her note on at the auto parts store! He showed me the copy he made and that sealed it. I could recognize Lianne's writing.

So how cool would it be, God, if that Lincoln would impact my Pastor-friend, this girl I can't stop thinking about, the guy at the auto parts store, and who knows who else? Whoever Rita Pennyworth is, she had to be affected, too! And then the atheist Matt, and Mary Parkinson? What are you doing, God?

Requests:
1. Praise You for your awesomeness. Help me learn to praise You more.
2. Bring Lianne and Dave this Sunday so they can hear Preston's sermon.
3. Help Preston more with that sermon. I think it's going to be his best ever.

4. If you can do all this with $5, God, I am going to start trusting You with $10/wk.

Wow, that last one sounds lame when I write it out. Gotta start somewhere, though. After all, it answers prayer #5.

Amen.

August 30, 2015
I wanted to start going to the Sunday school class today to learn more, but I had to come to Preston's office and write this down. Preston and I were praying this morning and my heart was pounding. He pulled up and saw the grass was not mowed and how bad the building looked on the outside and just about had a fit. He said people needed to know we cared enough to be ready for them when they showed up. I was thinking about how no one ever shows up that hasn't already seen the building and he saw it in my eyes.

I just told him to come with me and started praying for the church. By the time we had walked through the building and went outside, Preston was spiritually tearing his clothes and sprinkling ashes on his head. I was so moved that I grabbed his hand and stopped and prayed over him like I've never prayed before. That You would move mightily in him, that someone would see what Preston sees, that the leadership would join us in our prayers for the people, and that You would bring every person who needed to hear Your message today.

Then we heard a car door slam. Guess who it was? (Like You don't know…) James Randolph got out of the car. *Dressed in casual clothes!* Next Vaughn Pinckney is going to show up in blue jeans. And that's not all. James went right to the shed and mowed the lawn. When we heard the tractor start up, we were walking in the back of the building. We just started laughing and praising God. That engine was the best worship music we'd heard all week!

Then as we walked through the back door and into the sanctuary, I met Blaise and Seth coming in from the front. As she went to the altar, Seth came to me and Preston and asked if we minded them praying together. I offered to pray with them, but Seth shook me off. Preston said he would go into his office and pray. I turned and went into a class room and prayed. When I came back out, Preston was standing at his office door shaking his head. I turned to look and there was James, kneeling with those teenagers and praying the sweetest prayer over them!

That's not all. As James went to talk to Preston, Seth and Blaise asked me to talk with them. They came before their parents on purpose, because they needed to pray about what to do. Turns out Blaise had talked to this woman named Rita and was convinced to keep her baby. Did I question if prayer was enough? She had to talk to that woman right around the time we were asking You to intercede for her!

Then I found out somehow Seth had run across *that same five-dollar bill!* In fact, Blaise gave it to the woman before she left.

Rita? Pennyworth? The same woman who gave it to Pastor? Is that possible?

I need to stop writing and go out to practice. But I'm wondering. What are you doing, God? And how can I be a part of it?

Requests:
1. That You continue to make me aware of You.
2. That You help me acknowledge Your presence and Your power.
3. That You help me say with my Savior, "Not my will, but Yours be done."
4. That You help me teach the congregation to celebrate!
5. That You show me what You can do with my $10/wk.

I can't wait for the service. Is this what revival feels like? I love it!

No way I'm saying Amen here. Don't want this prayer to end!

P. S. Note right before service – James asked to pray with us every Sunday morning, and he's going to ask Will and Vaughn to join us. Another answered prayer. Preston was right. This prayer journal stuff is amazing!

VAUGHN

Grimacing, the sole elder of Beulah Community Church looked for a loophole. He felt flushed as he read the Scripture Pastor Preston was teaching and tried to see it from a different angle. Under the table, his long legs uncoupled and he started tapping his right foot. Flipping back, he picked up in verse one and read the first eighteen of chapter nine. Once again smoothing the white wings at his temples, he straightened his tie and then raised his hand.

"But, Pastor," Vaughn said. "Isn't Paul making the point that he isn't accepting the support?"

"Absolutely," Preston responded, smiling. "And, actually, I teach this only to get to verse nineteen."

Preston started to look down at his Bible, but pretty Mary Parkinson interrupted his return to the Word. "But that doesn't change the fact that it says here the Lord *commanded*."

Vaughn's grimace deepened. "Where?"

"Verse fourteen," Mary said. Vaughn's foot stopped tapping, instead balancing on his toes so his heel could pump up and down fast enough to make his chair move.

She was right. Though Paul was boasting that he was choosing not to use it, he taught that preachers of the Gospel had the right because of the Lord's command.

In the same way, the Lord has commanded that those who preach the Gospel should receive their living from the Gospel.

Why hadn't he read that before? Maybe he had, and because of the context discounted it. Vaughn rubbed his clean-shaven chin as he turned the thin page back and then forward again. A reference directed him to Luke 10:7. Jesus talking, saying the worker deserves his wages. He looked up at Preston and back down.

What was his game? Was he trying to milk the church for more money? Why bring this up now? Vaughn waited for Preston to go on, but he let the teaching hang in the air. Unnerving, how he always knew when to stay quiet. So many of their former pastors had been so busy teaching they forgot they had students. This one seemed to sense when something important was happening without his help. Was that manipulating? Or was it letting the Holy Spirit lead?

"I agree with Mary," Will said. Vaughn shot him a look and saw James nodding. His two deacons were buying it hook, line, and sinker. Well, Preston was going to find this fish had more fight in him yet.

"But Paul seems to be saying it is more spiritual not to accept the support," he said.

"Oh, I agree," Preston said. "Paul is making a point here that has nothing to do with pay. He's saying despite the fact that he could call that in, he's choosing not to for a reason. What's the reason?"

"A reward," Dolores Joyce said. Vaughn looked over at the oldest member of Beulah Community Church. Was she buying it, too?

"What reward?"

Pages rustled after Preston's question. Mary cleared her throat. Vaughn tried to clear his mind. The answer was in verse eighteen, so he didn't have to think about it. Instead, he concentrated on how to counter this masterful stroke.

How had it come to this? For 22 years he had been an elder of Beulah Community. He was there in the heydays, there when the pastors fell. They always fell. The last four were proof enough of that. Vaughn tightened his neck muscles and gritted his teeth as he thought of Charles. Back then they had four elders, but for some reason, Pastor Charles was always fighting with him. The other three weren't much more than yes men. He'd ask to change something and they would say yes. Vaughn felt he had a duty to play devil's advocate. Why hire a youth minister or a worship leader? Why should the elders do some of the teaching? Why did they need a secretary?

When Charles blew up at Vaughn in a congregational meeting, the pastor was surprised they sent him packing. Vaughn wasn't. He'd known going in that support for the pastor was declining. What he didn't expect was how many people left with him; even people Vaughn was sure voted him out. Two of the elders stepped down, but no great loss there.

The same had been true of Ben when he was seen leaving the home of his sweet young secretary — what was her name? Elena — at seven o'clock in the morning. He had no idea he was about to be fired.

They both denied any wrongdoing, but that didn't matter. The appearance of evil, and all that. Not only did that signal the end of Ben's ministry, it also proved Vaughn's point about having a secretary. Too much bad could happen letting a young pastor spend time alone with a woman in the office.

Wayne was the perpetrator of his own demise. Two services, indeed. How were they going to keep track of everyone? How could they feel connected as a family? When Wayne accepted another pulpit, most of the new people left. That included the last elder from the days of Pastor Charles as well as the new elder they had recently ordained. Vaughn stayed and soldiered the congregation through.

At least Henry had the decency to leave on his own. As soon as they realized they could no longer pay him full time, Vaughn knew his days were numbered. Henry had been a pastor all his life and hadn't done much to prepare for his retirement years. He couldn't exist with part time pay, felt he was too old to find a full time job and be a tentmaker. Vaughn and his two deacons, James and Will, gave him the choice. Henry resigned.

Which was why Vaughn was struggling with this passage. If this was the Lord's command, Henry had the biblical high ground. The whole conversation Vaughn had with Will and James convincing them to stand firm on their decision was wrong. They could have paid Henry another two years with their reserves in savings and certificates of deposit.

Sneaking a peek at James, Vaughn tugged at his collar and cleared his throat. "Pastor, the answer is in verse eighteen."

"Will you read it for me, sir?"

"Of course," he said. Clearing his throat again, feeling the blood rush to his temples, he read, "What then is my reward? Just this: that in preaching the Gospel I may offer it free of charge, and so not make use of my rights in preaching it."

"Thank you," Pastor Preston said. He scratched his goatee and looked around the room. "Perhaps you thought Paul would say he was looking for a heavenly reward. That God would love him more for doing it. That he believed it's what Jesus wanted for him. But no. He did it because he believed so much in the message he was willing to do it free of charge.

"That's how much I believe in it, too. Most pastors feel this way. We would do it for free. We do it for free when we are not 'working for the church.' That's why there's no such thing as a part time pastor."

Out of the corner of his eye, Vaughn saw James sit up and lean forward. Will was still lounging, but he looked much too attentive. This was not going well at all.

"Any person called by God is going to minister full time whether employed by a church, a grocery store, a warehouse, or Wal-Mart." Mary and Dolores chuckled at that. "I see some of your relatives work there," Preston said.

Will said, "Then why do we have full time pastors? What's the point of the church paying them?"

"So that they can concentrate on their calling," Vaughn said. He had to get out in front of this. "Less time working somewhere else means more time focusing on the business of the Gospel. Study time, community outreach, whatever the church needs. The less they have to worry about their livelihood, the more they can do for the Lord."

Preston smiled. "Well said. But as Mr. Pinckney noted, Paul is boasting that he is doing it for free anyway. The point of the passage is why he is doing it, and the answer is in the rest of the passage. Dolores, will you read for us starting in verse nineteen and continuing through verse 23?"

"I have the King James," Dolores warned.

"You have the Word of God, Dolores," Preston said.

Dolores smiled. "For though I be free from all men, yet have I made myself servant unto all, that I might gain the more. And unto the Jews I became as a Jew, that I might gain the Jews; to them that are under the law, as under the law, that I might gain them that are under the law; to them that are without law, as without law, (being not without law to God, but under the law to Christ) that I might gain them that are without law. To the weak became I as weak, that I might gain the weak: I am made all things to all men, that I might by all means save some."

"Thank you," Preston said. "Sum up what Paul writes here."

More shuffling, more page turning. Vaughn willed the color to drain from his face. This passage he knew. He had used it countless times to defend the importance of a small church. God blessed some of those other churches, but He also desired smaller churches that could teach things the bigger churches could not. Family. Connectedness. Biblical community. Get too big and the church risked losing those things. So God could very well be asking Beulah Community to remain small so He had an outlet for that kind of experience.

"Is he saying he changes for the circumstances?"

Preston met Will's question with an arched eyebrow and a glance around the room. "Is he?"

James scratched his nose. "Kind of. He also tells us he is still under the law for Christ's sake. So though he changes, he stays the same?"

"Yeah," Will said. "Like he's saying he tries to understand the people around him."

Biting his lip, Vaughn finally worked up the courage to look Preston in the eye. The young man met his gaze evenly. That's when he knew.

Preston wasn't bucking for a raise or a full time gig. He believed in his calling. He believed he was sent to Beulah. He would not quit. Not for money, not for prestige, not for trumped up accusations. Not for anything.

The air conditioning kicked on. Vaughn looked down at his hands on the Bible. He knew more than that. With sudden clarity, he saw what his hands had done.

"I have a story to share in the sermon today," Preston said, "about how God can use our culture to reach us in unexpected ways. I've been using Paul's second letter to Timothy for my personal study lately. I'm struck by his charge to his young protégé to preach the Word in season and out of season, to be patient and careful in how we teach it to people.

"So listen to me. This passage has nothing to do with how we treat our pastors financially. The lesson is way more important than that. Paul is saying some things are core, and some things are cultural. When we confuse the two, we limit the reach of the Bride of Christ."

"Pastor?"

"Yes, Dolores?"

"What's your story for the sermon today?"

Preston laughed. "Now, young lady, you know I don't like to spoil the sermon during class. You might decide to leave before the service!" Everyone chuckled. Dolores smiled. "It was worth a try."

"Let's just say I was blessed by a five-dollar bill this week."

James looked up quickly, then at Dolores. Dolores' eyes were as big as saucers, but she said nothing. Vaughn knew a story when he saw one, but the pastor had missed that exchange. He was reaching down to grab a pile of paper.

Preston passed out a sheet with a list of things the church did running beside two columns of boxes to check. The first column had "Core" at the heading, the second column had "Culture" atop it. As they went through the list, Vaughn felt something rising in him.

Shame? Guilt? Anger? Frustration? Fear?

Whatever it was, he didn't like it. Excusing himself, he fled the classroom into the hallway, across the sanctuary where Jason practiced a new song, through the foyer into the tiny bathroom.

He couldn't know the irony of finding an epiphany before the same mirror where Pastor Preston found his days before. Only the Spirit was *present* in that *moment*, an eternal witness to each. As the young man had done earlier, the elder let the tears of sanctification flow.

WILL

I couldn't help myself. When Vaughn got up and ran out of the classroom I turned and looked at James. He winked at me. Winked! I had to work hard at controlling the smile on my face. What was God doing? First James shows up in a golf shirt and slacks, then Vaughn gets a dose of reality on the same morning?

What was happening?

Maybe I should explain. My name is Will Dunham, and I'm the newest member of the leadership team at Beulah Community Church. We used to have a huge board that ran things, but not anymore. With only about thirty regularly attending, we now have Vaughn—our elder—James Randolph, and myself. We're deacons, and though we outnumber our elder we would never think of going against what he believes is right for the church. He's been in more spiritual scrapes than James and I put together. He's forgotten more about leading the church than we've learned.

I respect that man.

So when James pointed out that Vaughn had stopped giving his tithe after he returned from his summer vacation, I was angry with my fellow deacon. So what if he decided to take a break? Maybe he had some extra bills when he got back, or a big purchase to make. I told James it was none of our business.

After six weeks, though, I had to admit something was up and it wasn't good.

We have this new preacher, Pastor Preston. No, wait; let me back up. Last summer, we made a leadership decision to step our pastor, Henry Whitman, down to part time. When he resigned, we were pretty surprised. I'm the youngest of the three of us, just turned forty last year, but I don't think even Vaughn saw that coming. None of us are very good at speaking in public, so when he left we were in need of a quick fix. Problem was we didn't want to hire someone full time and we didn't know how much we could afford after some people left in protest.

Nine months we tried to find somebody. That's when Preston stepped in. He was a young guy, not long out of seminary. Vaughn told us that's what we'd get for our money — a kid who needed some practice preaching until a larger church snatched him up. He was right that no one else wanted the job. He was wrong about Preston.

That boy wanted to be at Beulah. Felt like God had called him there. One of the advantages we have as a small church is that we still have a parsonage. His family moved in, his wife found a job, and Preston started preaching.

The very first sermon, James and I knew he was going to be different. He told us God spoke in continuity, so he wanted to start in the Old Testament and work through the cross to the church in Acts. I loved Henry, but I don't think he did more than five sermons from the OT.

Then Preston told us we were going to spend a lot of time asking ourselves why. Why is this passage in the Bible? Why is God sharing this part of history? What does it mean for us today?

Wow. I told my wife, Sara, we were in for a ride. I wasn't wrong. Preston seemed to get better every week. Then our organist passed away. Sad day, that. She had been playing since before Sara and I joined the church back when Ben was the preacher. Such a lovely spirit. Unfortunately, no one else in the congregation knew the organ. We had one teenager who could kind of plink away at a piano and Jason, who knew how to play guitar. The teenager bowed out after the first Sunday. The second Sunday, Jason started playing. He's been the main guy ever since.

I miss the organ, to be honest. But the guitar is okay. Where was I?

Oh, yeah. James and I did some probing and realized Vaughn was having issues with Preston. Nothing big yet. Nothing like whatever happened with Pastor Charles. Preston was madly in love with his wife and so no hint of character problems like Ben. Weeks when the church didn't bring much at offering, Preston refused to be paid. No financial stress like with Pastor Henry. He preached the Word, was a praying young man, and he started teaching us things we had forgotten about following Jesus.

So why was Vaughn not giving?

My thoughts were interrupted by the end of the class. Vaughn had not returned to his seat. As we helped Preston gather up the papers and put away the borrowed Bibles, he asked me if I knew where Lance Dawson was. I told him I thought I did because his twins had been at the church this morning when I got there.

"Still?"

"What do you mean?"

James smiled. "Blaise and Seth prayed with me today. I think she's come to grips with her condition."

"Oh," I said. "Well, they told me they had to go home and talk to their parents together so I shouldn't expect the Dawsons for class."

"Praise God," Preston said. Then his eyebrows pinched between his blue eyes. "Can you guys do me a favor?"

"Certainly, Pastor," James responded.

"Can you find Vaughn? I'd like the three of you to pray for me this morning. Maybe I'm crazy, but I think today is going to be a big day and I want to be ready for my sermon."

I told them I'd find him. James and Preston went toward the church office and I went in search of Vaughn. He was at the front door, looking out the glass at the parking lot.

"Dawsons are here," he said.

"Yup," I answered.

"Who is that?"

I held my tongue and looked where he pointed. Two men got out of a beat up old Ford economy car; a scruffy-chinned guy with darker coloring and a rough, athletic guy with sandy blonde hair.

"I can't believe my eyes," I heard a female say. I turned to see sunlight dancing in Mary Parkinson's eyes. "He meant it."

She brushed past me and Vaughn and opened the door, running out to the sidewalk toward the parking lot. I heard her say "Dale?" as she stopped. He smiled and so did the man with him. They walked up and he was trying to introduce the man who came with him, but Mary leaped into his arms to give him a hug. He staggered back. We couldn't hear it from inside, but he was laughing and grinning from ear to ear.

"Vaughn?" My elder turned to me. "Pastor asked us to pray for him in the church office before service starts."

"Who will greet for us?"

I smiled and looked out the window. "Mary is doing a fine job."

"I guess she is," Vaughn replied. "Okay, let's go."

We waited to shake Lance's hand so he didn't think we were turning away from him and his family. He was smiling and looking over his shoulder where his wife was hugging Blaise. Lot of that was going on this morning.

"Hey, brothers!" Lance shook Vaughn's hand and looked back at the parking lot. "I bet that's the fella Mary met online!"

Wow, the world sure has changed.

After we exchanged pleasantries with the rest of the Dawsons, Vaughn asked Lance to man the door and gave him some bulletins. Lance agreed, then stepped in and whispered something in Vaughn's ear.

Breaking into a grin, Vaughn gripped the younger man's hand and smiled warmly. Nodding at him, he pulled Lance into an embrace. I almost passed out. Vaughn Pinckney, hugging a man in public?

Before I could comment, he was leading me into the sanctuary. Dolores was in her seat, joined by a man who was sitting in Chet's old spot. Was that Klaus Knable? The Robinsons were there, too, over on the right three pews back. Some of the other families were already in their spots, too. Wow. I guess Pastor Preston can remember who to pray for during the week just by going through the pews and thinking about who sits where.

We passed the sound booth where Jason was making final changes to his sound board and I told him I'd be back to run it soon. In the hallway beyond the double doors, we turned right and went to the church office. Once I stepped inside, he closed the door and turned to the two men waiting for us. We took our seats as if we were having another leadership meeting, except instead of shuffling papers we shuffled feet and hands. We had to meet in that office. Pastor Preston's cubbyhole didn't have enough room. I don't know why, but in that moment I felt uncomfortable about it.

"Thank you, gentlemen," Preston said. "Like I was telling James and Will, Vaughn, I would love to have you pray over me this morning . . ."

Vaughn raised a hand for silence. Preston gave it to him. The two men held gazes for what seemed like an eternity. Only a moment, but so much was happening I couldn't keep track. Finally, Vaughn broke and looked down.

"Pastor, before I can do that, I want to announce my resignation."

I don't know which one of us said what because we were all talking at once. We can't let you do that, Vaughn. We need your experience. The church would be lost without you. Are you leaving the eldership or the church? We had so many questions that we couldn't wait for his explanation. He held up his hand again and waited for our silence.

"Preston, I don't know if you are the right man for this job." I started to protest, but Vaughn said, "Let me finish, Will." He looked back at Preston. "I don't know if you are the right man for this job because it's going to take a lot of work to fix what I've done.

"I have been an elder in this church for so long," he said, then his voice broke. James put a hand on his shoulder. "Too long. At some point, I forgot what I was supposed to be doing. I wanted to protect the church. That's my job as an elder. But at some point, I started believing BCC was more important than the mission.

"I haven't liked you from the beginning, Preston, because you have been trying to show me that since you got here. This morning, God let me know He agrees with you."

At that point, Vaughn didn't have to ask for silence. There was so much silence, it filled the room and threatened to spill out into the sanctuary, into the parking lot, into Beulah, threatened to cover the world. I wasn't breathing.

"I left the church months ago," Vaughn continued. "James. Will. You both know I stopped tithing. You've been good enough friends not to press me about it, but your questions let me know you noticed."

We both shrugged uncomfortably. James nodded.

Vaughn said, "I just can't do it anymore. I'm tired of fighting. God wins. I don't know if that means I'm supposed to find another church, but I know it means I'm supposed to stop trying to control this one. I love you, James. You are the leader this church needs. Along with Pastor Preston. Will, you're going to be important, too."

I looked over at Preston and saw tears on his cheeks. That kid cries at the drop of a hat.

Leaning in, grabbing the hands of James and Preston, Vaughn closed his eyes and bowed his head. I held the other hands of those two men, but I couldn't bow my head. I sat there staring at them as Vaughn started asking for forgiveness and asking God to lead us as we lead the church. He prayed for Preston's sermon, for Jason's music, for the hearts of the people who were there and that others would come and see what God was doing at BCC. When he finished, James started. By the time he finished and it was my turn, there was nothing left to pray.

So I just said, "God, may what my brothers prayed be heard by you. Amen."

Then we all stood up and hugged each other. James made some joke about getting Vaughn's parking spot and the tension broke. My elder told James he better never give up the spot he has because people were coming and they were not ghosts or super heroes. I didn't understand that, but I laughed with them anyway. As I followed those two out, I turned back to see Preston drop to his knees and thank God for His provision.

Then I walked down the hall to the sanctuary and stopped in my tracks.

LANCE

On the one hand, passing out bulletins was the last thing he wanted to do today. On the other hand, the job gave him an excuse to look for Jack. Watching Mary shyly separate herself from the man she had been courting online the last few months, Lance Dawson thought of another bonus. He got to see any visitors who came. Vaughn liked to joke that they never came, but Lance knew better. About every other week somebody showed up. They just didn't stick around very often.

Lance believed Pastor was going to change that. Getting baptized by him had been an honor since Preston was the first to challenge his obstinance about it. He still remembered what the pastor said.

"Lance, Jesus was baptized, disciples were baptized, disciples baptized others, and all over the Bible, we hear about baptism. Whatever you believe about it, you can't believe it doesn't matter."

Pastor dunked him the following Sunday.

Opening the door for Mary, Lance heard her say, "You are kidding me!"

"No," Dale said. "I gave it to Chris. I wanted to ask for it back so I could give it to you." The other man said, "And I'm sorry, I didn't know Dale wanted to ask me for it. I gave it to a waitress named Hope."

"That's me."

The three of them turned around, surprised. Lance felt strangely outside the experience. He thought, maybe, so did Dale and Mary. Chris only had eyes for the young lady behind them. She was pretty, much shorter than Chris, but obviously there to see him. Instead of moving toward her, though, he took two steps back. Dale stepped forward and held out his hand.

"I'm Dale."

She shook his hand and smiled, then looked back. "Which one is this?"

"Everyman," Chris said, then turned on his heel and shouldered Lance out of his way to get inside. The three of them watched him disappear into the sanctuary.

Dale asked, "Is there a back door?"

The young lady fiddled with a wrist brace. "I'm so sorry. I shouldn't have come."

"Yes, you should have," Mary said, putting an arm around her. "Men don't like surprises, even when they are good. Come on, I'll show you around."

As she ushered the girl inside, Dale walked up and shook Lance's hand. "Good thing women like them."

"I don't know," Lance said, smiling at the man. "Some women like them. My wife would rather know what's coming. I'm Lance."

"Dale."

"Welcome to Beulah Community."

As the visitor followed the other three inside, Lance looked back out into the parking lot. Still no sign of Jack, although another car had pulled in. Thinning hair, wide face, blue jeans and a shirt that advertised *In Style Salon*. Was that Owen Taylor? Lance smiled when Owen finally got to the door.

"Didn't expect you to be here," Lance said.

Owen laughed. "I don't know how to take that, Lance."

"Warmly, brother! I just know you are usually over at St. Michael's."

"True," the man said. "I guess I'm here because of Mary."

"A lot of that going on."

He shook the man's hand and then watched as Owen made his way to the sanctuary. Klaus Knable was coming into the foyer and headed for the bathroom. Lance smiled, thinking of the story Seth had told. His boy had no idea what kind of impact he had on the people around him.

The thought brought him back to that morning, sitting around the coffee table in the living room. Listening as Blaise confessed she was the one Seth was giving money so she could end her pregnancy. Lance had known. Who else would Seth save a bunch of money to help? What other situation would have created Seth's moral dilemma?

Knowing had caused Lance to write on that Lincoln that *God is real*. He hoped Blaise would see her dad's handwriting and think twice about the decision. Turned out she never saw it because she was so nonplussed about Seth's addition on the front.

Then this woman Rita, then Uncle James praying with her. He had so many people to thank, so many reasons to praise God this morning, he couldn't wipe the grin off his face. Another car pulled in the parking lot as he welcomed the Petersons, the Smiths, and the Alexanders. When Mister Knable came out of the bathroom, Lance walked over and held out his hand.

"Mister Knable, what a surprise! Do you remember me?"

The old man looked at him from under bushy eyebrows, then shook his head.

Lance handed him a bulletin. "I worked at the auto parts store for Dave Graybill about two years ago when I lost my job."

"Ach," the man said. "My apologies, sir."

"No problem," Lance replied. "You might know my son better. Seth Dawson?" The little man's eyes lit up. "He is the one I am here to see!"

"Thank you for your help," Lance said.

"I am pleased to honor the father of that fine boy. He is a gem."

"Yes, he is. Do you need help finding a seat?"

"I have already been welcomed by a beautiful young lady named Dolores," Klaus said. "I told her I would sit by her as long as I am near the aisle so that if I must stand or leave I can do so without interrupting the service."

The man went inside and Lance looked up. He couldn't believe his eyes. Two more cars were pulling into the lot. When was the last time they had seen this many people?

Still, no sign of Jack. A young girl got out of the driver side of an old Ford Taurus that was puffing exhaust as it stopped. She went to the back seat and unstrapped a toddler as another woman exited the passenger side.

Rita.

Somehow, Lance knew. He forgot his post. Walking briskly toward them, his nice blue jeans swishing with every step, the heat bearing down on him despite some cloud cover, Lance marched toward her. As he took the last three steps he realized how threatening he probably seemed. She was a black woman in the parking lot of a predominantly white church and this man was striding toward her with purpose. Shrinking back a bit and pulling her purse in front of her chest, she watched with wide eyes as he stepped up to her and embraced her, squeezed her tightly, lifted her off the ground.

"Oh, sweet Jesus," she grunted, then started laughing. "Brother, you gonna have to put me down!"

Lance did, then drew back. "Blaise is my daughter, and you are Rita."

She nodded. "She told you."

"God sent you and my son to her. Thank you."

The younger lady laughed. "God sends Rita to a lot of people. Does Jason go to this church?"

"The guy who leads our worship?"

Rita laughed and looked at her friend. "I told you he wasn't just trying to impress you, girl!"

Smiling, she led the little curly-headed one around the car and shook Lance's hand. "I'm Lianne, and this is my daughter Caitie. Rita wanted to introduce me to your daughter because I've been where she is."

Lance put his other hand on his forehead. "I can't stand it. It's like God is answering all our prayers in one morning!"

That's exactly the moment Lance looked up and saw Jack Ilsey stop his Mustang in the parking lot. Chuckling, he excused himself from the two women and went over to his buddy's car. He got to the window just as David Graybill and his family pulled up. Lance recognized Tess in the back seat of their car. Blaise would be excited to see another teenager, a friend, at the church. He waved at his former boss and then looked down.

"Hey, dude," Jack said. "I don't want you to get the wrong idea."

Lance reached in and put a hand on his friend's shoulder. "What wrong idea?" "Don't expect me to get all religious."

"I won't, man. I promise."

Jack sat in the car, gripping the steering wheel and looking with dread at the church building. Lance was seeking the right words as David got out of the car and crouched to wave at them from Jack's passenger side.

"I didn't know he'd be here."

"Me, either," Lance said. "I guess the church takes all kinds."

Jack snapped his head around, searching his friend's eyes for any trace of mockery. He found none. Relaxing a little, he shook his head and took the car keys out of the ignition.

"Come on," Lance said. "You can sit in the back with me."

Another car pulled in, the driver a teenager with blonde hair and a lip ring. Lance waved at him, but he just glared. Shrugging his shoulders, he stepped back to allow Jack to exit his car. They walked toward the church building and went inside. The service was close to starting, so Lance led Jack in to find the rest of the Dawsons and sat him with them. As he was returning to his post, he saw Vaughn, James, and Will step out of the back hallway and stop in their tracks.

Lance laughed and went to his brother-in-law. "What's the matter, James? Haven't you boys been praying for people to come?"

Behind them all, Will said, "Sweet Jesus."

Yes, indeed. Lance went back to the front doors and handed out bulletins to recent arrivals. When the music started and the flow dissipated, Lance shaded his eyes from the sun breaking through the clouds. Whoever the teenager was, he still sat in his car. Not wanting to miss a moment, Lance waved the young man forward. Nothing. Shrugging, he turned and walked toward the sanctuary. Jason was leading the people in singing Amazing Grace. How appropriate for this day.

Pastor Preston stepped into the sanctuary and looked at Lance, bewildered. He grabbed James Randolph and pulled him back into the hallway. Lance noticed his pastor was clutching something in his hand. Notes for the sermon, maybe? As he walked toward his seat, he got a better look.

A photocopy of that five-dollar bill was on the top.

DISBELIEF

"I can't believe my eyes," Mary said. Her heart leaped in her chest. "He meant it." She brushed passed Vaughn Pinckney and opened the door, running out on the sidewalk. Just shy of the first parking block, she stopped. Was she sure? Mary only had one picture of him. "Dale?"

He smiled, scratching nervously at his beard, and she was certain. Half turning, he gestured toward the man beside him. She didn't care. As he stammered something about Chris, she ran the last three steps to him and leaped into his arms. He staggered back as he caught her, spinning her in the air to keep his balance. Throwing his head back, he laughed.

"You act surprised," he said, setting her on her feet.

"I guess I didn't believe you."

He grinned. "Believe me."

For a moment, they studied each other's faces. He was younger than she imagined. She was more beautiful than her picture. The man with Dale cleared his throat uncomfortably, but when they turned to him he was smiling, too.

"Three is a crowd," he said. Dale and Mary talked over each other to say how sorry they were, but he waved them away. "No, no, don't apologize."

"Mary, this is Chris."

"Were you the friend crazy enough to come with him all the way from Alabama?"

Chris shrugged awkwardly and looked at his feet. Dale rescued him by saying, "No, Mary. He's a new friend I met here."

She noticed the grateful look on the other man's face and knew she had stumbled on a story. Not wanting to drag it out of them—they would tell her when they were ready—she instead addressed why Dale was standing in her church parking lot this Sunday morning.

"Dale, I'm sorry I made you worry. Turns out your trip was for nothing."

"Meeting you in person isn't nothing, Mary," he said.

She smiled, then wrinkled her brow. "I mean the reason you decided to come. I lost that money."

"What money?"

"The five-dollar bill that got me all worked up." Dale smiled and looked at Chris, but she plowed on before he could interrupt. "I put it in the front pocket of my purse and went to see the owner of my salon the following morning. I know I put it there, but it was gone when I got home. I had a chance to do something important, but I blew it."

"I can't believe it," Chris said.

"What?" Mary looked from one man to the other and saw wonder on their faces.

Dale held out his arm for her. She took it and let him lead her up the sidewalk toward the church. For a few steps, he said nothing. Just as she was about to ask again, he looked up at her.

"When I came to Beulah, I couldn't find my hotel. I had forgotten the car charger and my cell phone died. I didn't have directions, didn't have a way to call anyone. So I stopped at the Buck Apiece store to get some food and ask directions." He looked at his friend. "When I got change, your Mister Lincoln was a part of it. That's where I met Chris." "You can tell her."

"Thanks," Dale said. "When I got out into the parking lot, I saw him standing there and I swear the Spirit nearly spoke aloud to me, telling me to go to him." "I'm a wanderer," Chris said softly. "I was lost and this man came up to me. He knew I was homeless somehow. God, I guess? So he came to give me that five dollars."

Dale pressed his arm against his side, a small hug to her interlocked forearm. "So your money did ministry without you."

"I'll say," Chris said. "It was the second time that five dollars came to me." "What?" Dale and Mary said together. Dale chuckled and said, "You didn't tell me that."

"I was the one who originally used it in that store. I found it in a dumpster behind a shopping strip."

"Was there a hair salon in that strip?"

Chris looked at Mary quizzically. "I think so."

Lance Dawson was holding the door for them as they entered.

Mary said, "You are kidding me!"

"No," Dale said. "I gave it to Chris. I wanted to ask for it back so I could give it to you." Chris said, "And I'm sorry, I didn't know Dale wanted to ask me for it. I gave it to a waitress named Hope."

"That's me."

The three of them turned around, surprised. Walking up to join them was a pretty young girl, chestnut hair and brown eyes. She was wearing a summer dress that got caught in the breeze as she and Chris stood gawking at each other. Dale finally stepped forward and held out his hand.

"I'm Dale."

She shook his hand and smiled, then looked back. "Which one is this?"

"Everyman," Chris said, then turned on his heel and shouldered Lance Dawson out of his way to get inside. The three of them watched him disappear into the sanctuary.

Dale asked, "Is there a back door?"

The young lady fiddled with a wrist brace. "I'm so sorry. I shouldn't have come."

"Yes, you should have," Mary said, putting an arm around her. "Men don't like surprises, even when they are good. Come on, I'll show you around."

Hope let Mary guide her through the door, but she stopped in the foyer. "I should go."

"What did you mean?"

"I mean I think I'm making Chris wish he was anywhere else."

Mary shook her head. "No, I mean when you asked 'Which one is this?'"

"Oh," Hope said. "When I met him at the restaurant, he introduced himself as Everyman."

"Why?" "Because he thought he was No One. I made him tell me his name, and he told me his story. When he left, he kind of thanked me for bringing the 'Chris' out of him but I could tell he was retreating back to 'Everyman.'"

Mary hugged her shoulders. "So you wanted to know which one you were meeting today."

"Yes."

"Come on," she said. "Let's go find *Chris*."

I couldn't believe it.

I should have run back toward the parking lot, but I didn't. I felt like I owed it to Dale to be at the church, so I ran inside. The foyer was a little crowded, so I went through the double doors on the other side. The main meeting room opened up before me, and people were everywhere. Lot of people for such a little church. I saw doors on my right and went through them. In the hallway beyond was a dead end to the right, so I turned left. About twenty feet down, it opened up into what looked like a mini-banquet hall. Some people were in there drinking coffee. There were three doors on my right. I went to the last one and opened it.

Inside was a little classroom with three long tables that formed a "U" and chairs along the outside. On a dry erase board was a quote from the Bible. *Therefore I do not run like a man running aimlessly; I do not fight like a man beating the air. –1 Corinthians 9:26*

I closed the door behind me and crash landed in a seat near the back, my breath coming in gasps. Running aimlessly, fighting the air: that was me. I put my head in my hands. This is not what I planned this morning.

I didn't think she would show up. I wasn't here to see her, but to honor a deal I made with Dale. Did I want her to be here? Wasn't I afraid she would show up?

The door opened, and there she was.

"Hi," she said, waving with the hand above her wrist brace. She bit her lip. Stunning.

"I can't believe you are here."

"Well," she said, walking forward and sitting in the first chair, "here I am."

"Why?"

She shrugged. "Because I told you I would."

"Why?"

"That's your favorite question, isn't it?"

I chuckled. "I guess it is."

"It's the question you've been asking God."

The temperature in the room rose a few degrees. She was wrong. That's the question I've been trying *not* to ask God. Why did I end up here? Why didn't I matter to Him? Why did He hate me so much?

I splayed my hands out on the table in front of me and looked at their weathered skin, the scars there. Coffee had stained the table near my left hand, and someone had written GV+BD in pen near my right. I wondered who they were. Anything to keep my mind off her, keep my eyes off her.

"Look at me," she said. I couldn't not obey. "I don't know the answers, but I know the question. Maybe if we ask the question, Chris can stay."

"Chris doesn't deserve it."

Hope smiled. "Everyman does."

Jason couldn't believe his eyes. He had walked up on stage to check the tuning on his guitar. When he turned, he was still looking down at the instrument, strumming lightly so he could hear it. Not until he looked up with the intention of nodding to Will back in the sound booth did he see her. She was sitting next to a black woman and Blaise Dawson, holding the cutest little girl he had ever seen. Lianne and the child wore matching T-shirts, hers saying *I have the best daughter in the world* and the baby's saying *I have the best Mommy in the world*.

He met her eyes and saw the challenge there.

Smiling, he stepped down from the stage and turned so he could push the guitar out of the way. He extended his hand, never taking his eyes off her eyes, and the little girl took it in both of hers. The room disappeared. All he could see was Lianne.

"Who is this pretty thing?"

After several seconds, the woman beside Lianne cleared her throat. "Child, the young man asked you a question."

Lianne's face softened and her eyes watered. "This is Caitie Beth."

Only then did Jason look at the little girl. "Hi, Caitie Beth. My name is Jason."

"Hewwo," Caitie said. They all laughed.

"I can't believe you are here," Jason said to her mommy.

Lianne's friend said, "I can't, either. Had to drag her by the scruff . . ."

"Rita!"

Jason laughed. "I have to start the service now, okay? Can we talk later?"

Lianne nodded.

Finding the stairs, Jason backed up onto the stage, unable to take his eyes off her for more than a moment. She was here. He felt the flush in his face and turned away, then looked up and mouthed thanks to God as he wondered why it had taken him so long to start that prayer journal.

"I cannot believe we are here," Bonnie said. She swept her hair back behind her ears to tighten her ponytail. She was wearing a dress, but she loved dresses. This one was modest, a dark blue that managed to bring out the smoky green in her eyes.

Eying her up and down, Matthew said, "Me, either. That dress makes me want to take you back home."

"Oh, husband," she responded in a false soprano. "Whatever can you mean?"

He barked a laugh, then turned to look at the squat little building. He had been mindlessly browsing Facebook the night before when he ran into a post from his co-worker, Mary. She had written about what it meant to her to be a Christian and he couldn't help himself.

He stalked her for a little while, found out what church she attended, then went to their website. The home page was actually pretty dynamic. The rest of the pages needed work. Eventually, Matthew had clicked on *Staff* and saw the preacher's picture.

Before he knew what he was doing, he was checking the time and the directions, sitting down on the bed beside his wife, and telling her he was thinking of going to church. She had made some caustic remark about how bad his migraine had to be and he realized with a start that it was gone.

Bonnie interrupted his reverie by asking, "Do you really want to do this?"

Matthew stared at the building. The guy at the door had disappeared. Through his open window, he could hear a bird chirping in a line of trees off to their left. He looked up at them, followed the branches of the tree to its trunk, followed the trunk down to the earth. The mud. The goo. He turned back to his wife.

"I think I do," he said. "But I don't want to go in right away. Don't they stand when they sing?"

Bonnie snickered. "Have you ever been to a church service?"

Matthew shook his head, looked out at the goo below the tree again. "We'll sneak in while they are singing."

"Well, I'm sure that's already started," Bonnie said. She opened her door and he followed suit. Around the front of the car, he held out his hand and she took it.

"I can't believe it, either, Baby."

"You're not going to believe this," Terry Berry said. She was sitting on the couch next to Spider. He was still high. "Hope just texted me."

"So."

"She went to church this morning."

"So."

Terry punched him in the arm. "Just surprised, is all. I'd be mad as a hornet at God if somebody stole all my Friday tips."

"Yeah."

"Vicky, you are one fine conversationalist."

"Don't call me that," Spider said. "And you don't want me for my ability to talk."

Terry laughed and reached for the needle and the rubber hose. "You got that right."

"You're not gonna believe how good this will make you feel."

"I can't believe this is the same church," Bobby Spaulding said. The parking lot was more full than he ever remembered it. His wife shook her head in disbelief. They had to park in the third row.

"Look, honey," Sally said. "James Randolph still parks in his spot in the back."

"Well, he had to today!"

"Come on. We're already late."

Bobby chortled as he got out of the car, but it cut off as he saw the car in the back of the lot next to the Buick James drove. He made himself continue closing his door, then walked around to the front of the car to join his wife. As he did, he grabbed her hand and pulled her close.

"What are you doing?"

"Don't look back," he whispered. "Chet's car is parked right next to James."

"No," Sally said, starting to pull away so she could find out if he was telling the truth. He grinned and pulled her back toward him, hoping his son didn't suspect they had seen him.

"I said don't look back there. He's still in the car."

She hugged him. "So that's where he went this morning. We thought he was going back to Victor's house."

"I know. I can't believe it."

LITTLE CHET

Hey, brother, I'm so excited for you. Two months in, right? You're past the worst of it, aren't you? To think the first time we met, you asked me to take you to that place.

Anyway, I found out from an officer what happened to you. Had to convince him I wanted to know for a good reason, but once I explained he was pretty cool about it. He thought I wanted to get some kind of revenge for what happened. How could I want to do that?

Zach, you may not realize it, but you changed my life that night. For good. If you hadn't wanted to go to rehab, if you hadn't crashed Spider's car, if you hadn't pushed that five-dollar bill in my hand, I don't know where I'd be.

So if you are wondering how I feel about our experience together, I can sum it up in two sentences.

1. I forgive you.

2. Thank you.

I hope hearing that makes it easier for you as you try to kick the habit. I hear one of the Twelve Steps is asking forgiveness from people you've wronged. Well, count me one less person you have to do that with.

Ever since my parents let me skip a grade when I was in middle school, I haven't been able to keep friends. Spider was the first one who made me feel like I could hang with him. Turns out he just loved making people feel as miserable as he feels. I tried to talk to him a couple of weeks ago, but he was too high to hear me. Maybe next time I'll take his cousin Jason with me. Jason is that guy that used to come to Spider's and hang with us sometimes, debating with us about God.

Anyway, since I skipped the seventh grade, people have been telling me how smart I am. I guess I know I'm smart, but the only thing it ever did for me was isolate me from the kids in school. Until now. I've been taking some online college courses about writing. I don't know if it will be a profession for me, but I might have a knack for it.

Which brings me to why I'm writing you. I was trying to think of a way to return the favor you did for me. In case you didn't believe me the first time, you changed my life for the better just by repeating over and over again, "My name is Hope." I can still hear your voice when I close my eyes. I thought you were crazy — and I guess you were — and had found some person named Hope who made you want to kick your habit.

But because you did, I found the real Hope. I wrote the story I included in this envelope about my experience the day after our accident. I hope my hope brings you hope from the real Hope.

282

The metal of the door handle was warm under my hand. That's when it became real. I stood there, not daring to look at my reflection in the glass because I knew I would bolt. Was I going to do this?

I was angry at myself. I mean, I had the same mental conversation in the car, outside the car, at the edge of the parking lot, and on the front walkway. I was tired of remaking this decision. Honestly, I also had the conversation with my parents and fought with myself in my room the night before as I blasted stuff on one of my RTS games, as I made myself some coffee and decided to read some, as I lay in my bed trying to sleep. I kept thinking at some point I would settle on it.

Was I really going to do this?

No one had seen me yet because the service was already in full swing. I didn't get to the church late; just couldn't leave the car. Ugh. I knew what to expect as soon as the door was opened. My parents used to go to that church and drag me with them back when Pastor Ben was there. Pastor Ben. Man, I haven't thought about him in years. He was old to me, but looking back he was pretty young for a preacher. We didn't have enough people to afford more than one pastor, so Pastor Ben met with the teens on Wednesday nights.

He was cool. He had this thing where you could bring in any music you wanted and challenge him to teach about God from it. Once, he did an Eminem song. Weird, huh? But he made it work. Then they said he was sleeping with his secretary and got rid of him. Crazy, that. No way he did that, but the guys in charge were so worried about what people would say that they let him go anyway.

Bunch of hypocrites. Half of them are divorced, you know. My parents went to another church out of protest. I thought that was pretty noble since they didn't know what to believe. I went with them to the new church twice and realized it was exactly the same as the church we left. Only no Pastor Ben. I quit going to church at all.

But they're about the same, you know? They sing songs, ask for money, do this thing called communion where they eat a dry little cracker and drink a swallow of grape juice that isn't enough to wash away the nasty cracker taste. Then they sing again, and then the preacher gets up and talks for an hour. Even with Pastor Ben, it seemed like forever on Sunday morning.

Anyway, there I was, getting ready to go in late. They would be into the third song or so, an upbeat tune because they try to get people pumped up before giving. Then they'd do a fourth song to slow it down to make people feel relaxed and reverent for communion. While everybody still has a bad taste in their mouths, the preacher gets up and reads from his manuscript or puts on his PowerPoint slides. After, he gives a lame altar call that has nothing to do with anything else he said, then they sing a song while no one goes up front. The pastor will say he knows people were affected by his words and will awkwardly pray for a better response next week and dismiss everyone. As if the level of pretension isn't high enough yet, the congregation files out past the preacher and tells him what a nice sermon it was, see you next week.

I knew what to expect, which is why I was standing outside wondering if I should wait until communion was over. I could slip in half way through the sermon, for that matter, and it would count. Make sure Gran saw me. Give her back the five dollars I told you about and tell her . . .

Tell her what? That God came through? That He got my attention? That her little five-dollar bill managed to return to me at the exact moment of the most critical event of my life? Zach, you gave me that five dollars right before you grabbed the wheel, remember? I remember, and I remember what I asked Granny a week before.

"Granny," I said, "if there is a God, He can use this five-dollar bill to reach me. Right?"

Standing at the front door of the church, I didn't know if God reached me or not. I just remembered sitting in the ER, waiting for the police to arrest me, crumbling that picture of Lincoln and opening it back up. Smoothing it out. Reading all the amazing things written on it under *In God we trust*. I pulled out and read every line again, though I had memorized them.

You can too, LC.
You can if you want to.
I do!
And He believes in you.
He is real.
He forgives wrong and blesses right.
Turn for a blessing.
Praise Jesus!
He told me
My name is Hope.

Every line was written by a different person, which made the whole message even more amazing. Like all those people were talking to me. Helping each other to get the point across to me. Unless . . . Unless . . . That would be weird, but I couldn't help wondering if it was only one author. I clenched my eyes shut.

"This better be worth it," I said, and opened the door. Guitar music met me in the foyer, people singing an old hymn, but kind of jazzed up. I remembered hearing it on my mom's Christian radio station.

See from his head, his hands, his feet
Sorrow and love flow mingled down.
Did e'er such love and sorrow meet
Or thorns compose so rich a crown?
O the wonderful cross, O the wonderful cross
Bids me come and die to find that I may truly live.

So they were already to communion. The foyer was way too small. I wanted another thirty steps to make the decision again, but two guys were standing in the middle of the room. One was older in a short sleeve polyester shirt and dress pants. The other one was younger, mid-twenties. He had a goatee and was wearing jeans and a decent shirt.

The young guy was saying, "I know we don't normally do it that way, but today is already kind of weird, isn't it?"

Then they realized they weren't alone and turned to look at me. The old guy mumbled something and walked into the sanctuary. The young guy walked over to me and held out his hand.

"Hello," he said, "I'm Preston."

"Hi, Preston," I said. He hesitated, expecting my name. I just looked at him.

"You okay sitting in the back?"

Was he serious? I nodded.

"Good, because it's full up front."

He opened the double doors and motioned me toward one of the back pews as the last verse was being sung. I looked left toward the stage over the backs of heads. Lots of heads. The last time I visited with my parents, thirty people were there and that old lady was banging on the organ. Had to be more than sixty people today and the guy strumming a guitar was Jason Nickerson.

Spider's Jesus Freak, never-do-nothing-wrong cousin. Seriously, dude, they are related.

I couldn't sit. I went to the back wall and nodded at the old guy running the sound. What was his name? Will? I stood and leaned back, clutching Lincoln and massaging the cotton in my hands. Was I in the twilight zone? I had seen Jason at Spider's a couple of times and assumed he was part of the scene. Maybe he still was, but I don't know if I ever saw him use. He just hung out with some of the teenagers who were too scared to try needles but didn't mind the bottle. Now I find him leading a church in a Christian song?

The last note died away and that young guy Preston walks up on the stage. He says, real serious, "I know those of you who were here last week are expecting communion right now. Please bear with me if from this point this Sunday doesn't seem much like any of the others."

Some people laughed a little as I watched, chin on my chest. This was the pastor? No way. Why didn't he say so when he shook my hand?

He seemed nervous because he was rubbing his hands together over and over. Then I saw he wasn't just nervous. He was excited, too. He stood there, kind of framed by the screen in the back where the words *This week's sermon: Real.* was projected.

"A few months ago, Jason and I decided we needed to pray more for our church. Every Sunday morning since, we've met early and walked through every room, between every pew, outside and around the grounds. We're asking God to show us what He wants us to do.

"I realized this morning we were already doing what He wants us to do. God wants His kids to talk to Him. Will you join me as I talk to Him? Just listen, and if you agree with something I say, feel free to say 'amen' out loud. Amen means *So be it,* so all you are doing is letting God and the people around you know that you believe what I am saying."

The room got real still. I almost laughed out loud. Bet they didn't see that coming. The preacher telling them they can talk to him? I thought it was different, anyway. When Preston bowed his head, everybody else bowed their heads with him. Except me. I watched.

"God, today is different and I think I know why. Please help me to do my best to explain why. I know You love us, and I know You want us to believe You are there. It's hard sometimes, God, because so often we can't see You. But I think we are going to see You today, God, and I'm praying everyone here gets a glimpse of how amazing You are."

He paused for a moment, like he was waiting for someone to say amen. No one did.

Everyone kept their heads down, including Preston. Then he lifted his face toward the ceiling. His eyes were closed. The stage was about fifty feet away, but do you know what I saw? A tear.

"God, You are awesome. You are amazing. You are loving. You are kind. You are gracious. You are real."

"Amen," said a black lady in the front of the room.

"You are patient. You are dangerous. You are present. You are Father."

"Yes," said a woman right in front of me.

"You are Son. You are Spirit. You are truth. You are love.

"My great desire is to represent You today. Help me do it clearly so others can know. Amen."

Everyone said amen after him, then they all looked up at him.

I thought he was never going to talk. He stood there looking at all the people. It should have been awkward, like when one of your classmates gets up to cite the Gettysburg Address and can't remember the first line. Or when you are forced to go to a school play and someone forgets their lines so completely that everyone knows it. But this wasn't that kind of silence. This is going to sound a little creepy, but it felt like this guy was waiting for everyone to be connected to him. Like each person's attention could link to him by a string and he knew he only had about twenty strings. Then he had a few more, and a few more.

Then, I realized he had my string. I rubbed that Lincoln and leaned in to hear what he was going to say.

"I'm a young guy. Twenty-four, just a year out of seminary — which I started late — with no experience leading a church. I'm a Christian — which I also started late, just six years ago — and don't have much experience living like one. When I put my faith in Jesus, I thought He fixed everything. I wanted to believe so badly that He would make everything work out right that I decided I'd make sure He knew how much I appreciated Him. So I became a pastor.

"I've got the education to be a pastor, but I'm not very good at it yet. In the same way, I've got the education to be a Christian, but I'm not very good at it yet. I still have days when I wonder if either one is true."

Okay, listen. That is not how preachers talk. Even if — especially if — it's true. People want their pastors to be Super Christians and have all the answers. I couldn't believe this guy was saying what he was saying. I couldn't help myself. I stepped away from the wall and walked around the end of the pew and sat down.

"I had one of those days this last Wednesday. I was working on this sermon. All I had was a few verses and a vague idea that I wanted to talk about taking the Good News of Jesus seriously. The sermon was going nowhere and I wanted to go anywhere else but here. I tried walking out here to get a fresh view. Know what I saw?"

I didn't, but I wanted to know.

"You. I saw you. Broken, hopeful, fearful, loving. And seeing you, I saw myself. Broken in my insecurities, hopeful because it was wrong to be hopeless if you know Jesus, fearful of the future despite singing *Blessed Assurance*, and doing my best to love people enough. Can you relate?"

"Yes," the woman next to me said. She was pretty, a little older than Preston. She sat by a guy who was a bit older than her who couldn't keep his eyes off her. Across from the two of them was a man I had seen walking around town the last couple of days, only he was all cleaned up. When I looked at them, they looked at me and the woman put her hand to her mouth like I startled her. I whispered an apology and tried to escape their creepy stares by concentrating on Preston again.

"Except I'm not supposed to see myself in you. I'm the guy who has all the answers. I'm the guy who is supposed to know the Bible forwards and backwards. Of all the people in this church, I'm the one that's supposed to have it together. It scared me. I started wondering if all this was worth it. Started wondering if I was the right guy for the job.

"I ran to the bathroom to splash water on my face and I heard someone pounding on the door."

"Yes you did," the black lady said, "because it was me!"

Everyone laughed, even the preacher. He shook his head, completely surprised. "You're Rita Pennyworth?"

"That's right," she said.

"Amazing. Thank you for your gift."

"Not my gift, preacher. God's gift."

"Okay, this can't get any stranger," Preston said, rubbing his goatee and looking down at his feet. When he looked back up I could tell he was trying to get ahold of himself. "I was asking what good is God if I can't even afford a haircut. I was asking what good is Jesus if I feel this hopeless sometimes. I was asking what good is church if there's nothing good about God and Jesus.

"I was asking for a miracle."

Zach, I wish I could describe what the place felt like right then. I mean, I wanted to know if he found a miracle. That's true. But it was more than that. It was like all those strings of attention tightened, at the same time they seemed to intertwine. I saw parents look at kids and wives look at husbands. I saw the lady next to me look over at the guy next to her. I saw a girl near the front look over her shoulder at the other guy in our row. I saw Granny turn to the man sitting on her right and wink. I saw my parents—I didn't even know they were coming—snuggle in close to each other. Like we were all making sure someone else was hearing this, you know?

"The knocking stopped. I looked at myself in the mirror and I didn't like what I saw there. Who am I to talk about God? Who am I to tell people about Jesus? Who am I to lead a church? I got so scared, I ran out of the bathroom and to the front door to leave. That's when I saw an envelope taped there by Rita P."

The old guy, Will? He was in charge of the screen. He clicked a mouse and the slide changed to show a scan of an envelope.

To: Pastor of Beulah CC
From: Rita P.

"Rita had been sitting in our parking lot, calling me, but I didn't pick up the phone. So she walked to the front door and banged on it while I hid in the bathroom."

"I knew you were in there somewhere," Rita said, and everyone laughed again.

"I watched her drive away as I opened the door and grabbed the envelope. Inside it were two things. This letter." Will was doing his thing again with the mouse. We saw the letter on the screen.

Pastor,
You don't know me, and I don't know you. I'm not
asking for anything. I was just challenged by a young
lady to give away this five dollars and I thought
maybe you could use it. Praying it blesses you.

Rita Pennyworth

"Oh my goodness," a girl sitting next to Rita said. I recognized her. Blaise Dawson, a cheerleader at our school. Real pretty girl who got knocked up. She turned to Rita and said, "The five dollars I gave you?"

"Yes, honey," Rita said.

"Wait," a young woman sitting on the other side of Rita said. "Five dollars? Was there writing on it?"

"Yes there was, Li," Rita said.

Pastor Preston cleared his throat and everyone laughed really loud. He acted like he was upset, but you could see this kind of amazement in his eyes. He shook his head again, smiling widely.

"Can anyone guess what else was in the envelope?"

Will didn't wait for everyone to guess, which was perfect. He pressed on the mouse and the image changed to the five-dollar bill Granny had given me. No lie. Same one. It had some of the words on it, but not all.

In God We Trust.
You can too, LC.
You can if you want to.
I do!
And He believes in you!
He is real.
He forgives wrong and blesses right.

Have you ever been in a room full of people and
something happens and it's like a conversation bomb goes off
in the middle of them? Seemed like suddenly everyone
wanted to talk. A few people turned to the person next to
them, pointing at the screen. Two people stood up. I couldn't
stand or point or talk. I felt thick as I looked into my hands
where old Abe Lincoln stared at me through the rest of the
words written around him.

Turn for a blessing.
Praise Jesus!
He told me
My name is Hope.
"That's it, isn't it?"

I turned to look at the redheaded lady sitting next to
me. She was looking down with wonder at the Lincoln in my
hands. When she looked back up at me, I nodded. Reaching
over, she squeezed my knee. I thought she was going to stand
up and tell everybody. Instead, she grabbed the hand of the
man next to her, bowed her head, and started silently moving
her lips.

Now that I think back on it, she was praying.

Somehow, the Pastor had regained control of the room. The strings were beyond taut now, like they are inside a piano, waiting for music to spring from them. My string was practically vibrating. I put my elbows on the pew in front of me, my chin in my hands.

"It gets better," the preacher said. "The mail had already been delivered, so I picked it up and flipped through it to find a circular from a local hair salon that had a coupon for a haircut. Know how much?"

"Five dollars!" The balding man down near the front on the left had shouted it out. "I know because it's my salon!"

Pastor Preston rubbed his hands again. "So God did three things for me. He gave me a haircut, renewed my faith, and sent me on a mission. I had to know the answers to my questions that day. What good is Jesus? What good is God? What good is the church?

"I went to the salon and . . ."

He stopped mid-sentence, staring at a guy sitting in the pew about two-thirds down on the right, close to the exit. I don't think he knew the guy was there until that moment. His jaw dropped and I could tell he had forgotten what he was going to say. The man nodded at him, stone-faced. The woman next to him was in a pretty blue dress that showed how red her face was getting.

"I—I'm sorry," the preacher stammered. "I feel like the Spirit is leading me to say this just as I was going to say it. But you are here. I'm sorry."

"It's okay," the man said. "I already know."

Preston scrunched his shoulders like he was working a kink out of his neck, then pulled at his goatee. Finally, he said, "I went to the salon and was confronted by a man who didn't believe in God."

Every head turned toward the guy, and his wife looked like she wanted to melt into the seat. He was red-faced now, too, but out of embarrassment. He motioned for the preacher to continue.

"He asked me some tough questions and I did my best to answer him. By the time he was done cutting my hair, I had so offended him that he wouldn't talk to me. I'm ashamed of that, but what happened next made it worse. I paid with this five-dollar bill and he thought I was trying to manipulate him.

"I wasn't. I was just using the blessing God had given me. Please forgive me."

The man nodded again, still stone-faced. Preston accepted it as forgiveness and turned to the rest of the congregation.

"I went back to the church and started notes on my sermon. It was very different than what I'm talking about this morning. I had a great idea with some awesome illustrations. I had a text selected that I thought was perfect. I was sure what I was going to say.

"Yesterday morning, I threw it all out. I started thinking about what it means for us to know Jesus, to follow His Gospel, to be the church. I remembered there was a passage in Hebrews that said *'Keep on loving each other as brothers,'* so I turned to it. The very next sentence, verse two of chapter thirteen, says, *'Do not forget to entertain strangers, for by so doing some people have entertained angels without knowing it.'*

"I thought about the contrast in those two. Love each other as brothers, entertain strangers. Which ones were likely to be angels? The strangers. And I thought about the strangers I had been affected by that week. The stylist. Rita. The cashier at Target. Had they been angels?"

"Lord knows I'm no angel," Rita said. Everyone laughed.

"Yes, sister," Preston said. "You were." She started to protest but he held up his hand. "The word in the Greek is *angelos* and it means messenger. You were a messenger of God that day when you gave me the money to get my hair cut. And when I went there, I was supposed to be the messenger for the man who cut my hair. And after, who knows if there is an angel working at Target?"

I didn't laugh at that. No one did. We were too busy trying to figure out where he was going.

"What I'm saying is we all have opportunities to be messengers for God. Sometimes we forget that. I read a Facebook post by a church member this week who asked some of the same questions I was asking. My hope is that she gets an answer from this. The church is meant to be a called out gathering of saints who are loving people better than anyone else on the planet; so much so, they become God's messengers with their lives.

"A little further down in the passage, the writer pens this: '*Remember your leaders, who spoke the word of God to you. Consider the outcome of their way of life and imitate their faith.*' That means I'm not supposed to be Super Christian. I'm supposed to be real. As I am real and learn to live by faith, I in turn show you how to live by faith. Then, as you learn how to live by faith, you show others how to live by faith.

"How can we do that? Look at the next verse when you get a chance. It says, *'Jesus Christ is the same yesterday, today, and forever.'*"

I couldn't follow it. I pulled back a little bit and so did the guy who cut the pastor's hair. But almost everyone else in the room leaned forward. I turned to look to my right and saw the wandering dude looking dead at me. He was so . . . lost.

"For those of you who hear me and understand, listen to another phrase written in this chapter. *'Through Jesus, therefore, let us continually offer to God a sacrifice of praise.'* For those of you I lost, let me explain. The writer of Hebrews realizes something as he describes what the church is called to do. We are, none of us, able to live continually by faith. We can be real if we want, but we can't be perfect.

"We've often been described by people on the outside as hypocrites, idiots, weak-willed, unintelligent, unaware of the progress of today's world, unable to come to grips with the truth of science and psychology. They think we blindly follow a religion that either shores up our self-esteem or strips us of our humanity; either presses us into slavery or covers our pride and arrogance. They think these things because from the outside they only see the failure of our God to bring about any significant change, any significant purpose to our lives. As Paul says somewhere in his writings, if the resurrection of Jesus is not true then we are to be pitied above all men.

"But what people on the outside don't understand is that we are not who they think we are and we do not think what they think we think. We are lost, but not from a shortage of self-confidence. We are a poor reflection of God, but not because we don't believe in Him.

"We are failures, but not because God is a failure. We are believers, but not because we are unaware of the advances of mankind. We just recognize something it is hard for every one of us to come to grips with. So hard, in fact, that we have to relearn it over and over and over.

"We are so lost that we've lost what we lost."

Preston paused and surveyed the room. I can't remember when I leaned back in, but we were all piano strings again. Even the stylist guy and his wife.

"Intellectually, philosophically, scientifically, psychologically, I — am — lost. And so are you. Broken by untrustworthy people, wandering away from any real idea of love, unwilling to give up what control I can exert over my life. The last thing I want to give up is that bit of control I have gained.

"So much so that I've forgotten this truth: control is an illusion. I can make nothing happen on my own, and what I can make on my own is nothing. So I look for a way to forget that, or reform that, or rephrase it where I can deny that truth. I don't want to be lost, so I convince myself that I am not. Until something happens I can't control. Until I rub against something that seems to be evidence that something else — Some*one* Else — might be in control.

"And I hide. Or rage. Or tremble. So many times we've been let down. By churches. By schools. By friends. By governments. By lovers and spouses. So often we have pinned our hopes on someone else and found out the truth that they are lost, too.

"Jesus alluded to this in a sermon He gave in Luke when He said, *'Can a blind man lead a blind man? Will they not both fall into a pit?'* So we are afraid to put our trust blindly in anyone. Not even if there is God.

"And that's why we have church. Because somewhere we have to learn how to be a beacon of hope for the rest of the world. A lighthouse, if you will. The storms are raging and we can't find safe harbor. Where can we go to find Someone Else who is in control and can save us?

"Which brings us back to Jesus. Every other religion tells us how good we ought to be in order for God to approve of us. Every person in the world knows on some level they can never be that good. So we either give up trying or give up believing. Jesus is different, though. He says, 'I see you in your pain, in your lostness, in your imperfection, and I refuse to leave you there.' So He died to set us free. And Jesus, as the writer of Hebrews tells us, is the same yesterday and today and forever. So if He loved us enough to save us before this moment, in this moment He loves us enough to save us still."

I stood up. The preacher looked at me for a moment, trying to decide what to do, deciding how to do it. I felt the lady beside me stroke my arm with her hand and then nudge me toward the aisle. I stepped out into open space.

Preston said, "May the God of peace, who through the blood of the eternal covenant brought back from the dead our Lord Jesus, that great Shepherd of the sheep, equip you with everything good for doing his will, and may he work in us what is pleasing to him, through Jesus Christ, to whom be glory for ever and ever. First by offering his salvation to you. Second, by gathering you together as the church. Third, by sending you out on mission. Amen."

Later I would learn he had quoted more of the verses from Hebrews chapter thirteen. I didn't hear it that way. I heard God talking to me, Zach, telling me He knew who I was and not only loved me anyway but trusted me with His work here on earth. I walked down the aisle with that five-dollar bill clutched in my fist. As I strode past Gran, I could feel her eyes on me and hear the sharp intake of her breath. When I knelt on the steps in front of the pastor, I could sense Spider's cousin rushing up and grabbing his guitar. He started strumming it and I recognized the tune for *Amazing Grace*.

I didn't cry, Zach. I didn't see the heavens part. I didn't see the face of Jesus or feel the Holy Spirit or start speaking in tongues. I just suddenly felt free.

"If God is speaking to you this morning as strongly as He is to this young man, I pray you will come forward and spend time in conversation with Him. James, can you and Will grab the communion trays? If you are a believer today, I invite you to experience for the first time again the love Jesus has for you. If you have just realized Jesus is someone you can believe in, Vaughn and I will pray with you and guide you through your next steps. Either way, let's make these words our prayer as we stand to sing."

Amazing Grace, how sweet the sound
That saved a wretch like me;
I once was lost, but now am found,
Was blind but now I see.

I didn't know what to pray, but I knew the truth of those words. I decided to follow the preacher's advice and make them my prayer.

DOLORES (REPRISE)

She couldn't stand. Her heart wouldn't manage. As Jason strummed the guitar to the opening notes of that faithful old hymn, she thought of Old Chet. Was he watching? Did he believe what just happened? Had God allowed him to be a part of what was happening today?

What were the chances? No, not chances. How much bigger was God than even she knew? Would she ever stop being amazed when He answered her prayers? Didn't she know by now how awesome her God was? She watched as Bobby and Sally joined their son. Smiled when she saw Blaise join the woman with the little girl and the nice black lady named Rita. Laughed when they were joined by the waitress and the wanderer, Mary and the man who had come to meet her. Others were joining them and Pastor Preston was kneeling to pray with each one in turn. Vaughn even knelt beside some of them on his old knees. Jason had to keep doing more verses as God did His business in Beulah Community Church. Then the worship leader sang a verse she hadn't heard before.

The earth shall soon dissolve like snow,
The sun forbear to shine;
But God Who calls me here below
Will be forever mine.

She saw Little Chet get up and turn, looking for her. When he saw where she was, he walked over and extended his hand. She reached up and as he took it in his, she felt a wad of paper.

"You were right, Gran," he said. "God can use this to reach me."

He released her hand and bent over awkwardly to hug her, then went back to his parents. They received him back with pride and Bobby asked if he could pray. As they bowed their heads, Dolores looked at what he had placed in her hand. Of course it was. Abraham Lincoln didn't wink at her as she smoothed him out, but he should have. Crisis of faith with a dead president, indeed.

Closing her eyes for a moment, she thought she could smell Old Chet's cologne. The memory was so strong, she reacted the way she always did in church. She reached out for his hand.

And felt skin. Opening her eyes, she looked down at the aging hand she was holding. Followed it over the cuff of the dress shirt, up the sleeve of the coat to the collar. Of course, Old Chet was not there. The man who looked at her was kind, though, respectful, his eyes lit up with joy.

"I'm sorry," she said.

"I'm Klaus," he responded.

Dolores held the five-dollar bill in one hand and Klaus's hand in the other and wondered what her Father could do with a twenty.

Made in the USA
Columbia, SC
08 November 2018